CAPE MAY SUNSETS

CLAUDIA VANCE

CHAPTER ONE

"Dave! Over there!" Margaret said pointing through the crowds on the beach.

Dave shielded his eyes from the bright, hot sun as he glanced ahead. "What is that? A mermaid?"

Margaret squinted to get a better look. "It looks like it ... right?"

Dave stared and nodded before glancing to his left. "Did you see the whale over there?"

Margaret craned her neck to get a better look, then took Dave's hand and led him through the people to the large blue whale. Dave stood in front of it and crossed his arms. "Well, this one is going to win. I'd put all my money on that."

"It's fantastic. The attention to detail is remarkable," Margaret said as she walked around the sculpture, then got sidetracked by another sand sculpture of a fish nearby.

A man who was sculpting the whale in the sand looked up at Dave with a smile on his face. "Glad you like it. I think this might be my favorite one yet."

"You do this a lot?" Dave asked, impressed with the art form.

The guy wiped his hands off and pulled two plastic knives

out of the pocket of his shorts and started adding some last-minute tiny details to the eyes. "I guess you could say that. Mostly just in New Jersey and Delaware, on the beaches of course. It became a hobby of mine years ago, and now I like to sign up whenever I get the chance."

Dave looked around at the hundreds of people standing on the beach, then at the thirty or so sand sculptures ranging in different themes, sizes, and colors. "This is something. I'm an artist myself. It's amazing what can be made into art … like this sand," Dave said as he reached down and grabbed a handful of sand, then let it slide through the cracks between his fingers. "I'm Dave by the way."

"I'm Wally. I'd shake your hand, but time's almost up. Gotta keep moving here. So, you're an artist, eh? Oil pants on canvas? Watercolor?"

Dave knelt down to hear him better. "Yeah. A little of this and that."

Wally nodded as he touched up some barnacles on the back of the whale. "Well, man. What I've found, personally, is if you're already an artist, you'd probably be good at this. There are a few tricks to the trade, though."

Dave laughed. "Oh, I don't know if this would be my thing, but it has got me inspired to start working on something again. It's been a few years."

Wally stood up and pushed his baseball cap closer to his eyes. "Inspiration can do a lot for ya, that's for sure," he said while putting his hand out for a handshake. "Nice meeting you, Dave."

Dave shook his hand and before he could say anything, a woman on a megaphone announced, "OK, everyone. The Cape May Sand Sculpture Contest is ending in five minutes. We ask that everyone get their votes in for their favorite sand sculpture now so we can choose a winner."

Margaret trudged through the hot sand to stand next to

Dave. "This is just too cool. We'll have to add this to our annual events to attend every year."

Dave put his arm around Margaret's shoulders. "Did you put a vote in for your favorite?" he asked as he glanced over at Wally, who had walked away to talk with a group of people.

Margaret smiled. "I did. There's an enormous sandcastle over there. A whole team of people worked on it," Margaret said pointing down the beach.

Dave scratched his chin. "Oh yeah? Guess I missed that one. I've been talking to Wally over here this whole time. I'm putting my vote in for him," he said as he walked over with Margaret to the people tallying the votes under a pop-up tent.

"One vote for the big blue whale over there," Dave said to the lady, who was sitting on a beach chair with a notebook under the tent.

"You got it," the lady said as she wrote something down on a piece of paper.

Margaret pulled her shirt away from her body as though to air herself out. "Can we just stay under this tent?" she asked half-jokingly. "The sun is brutal right now, but I want to stay and see who wins."

The woman got back on the megaphone. "OK, everyone. Time's up. Give us a few minutes to tally the votes, and we'll announce the winners! In the meantime, don't forget our hard-working water ice and ice cream cart vendors out here on the beach. Grab yourself and the family some cold treats and support the local businesses."

Dave nudged Margaret. "Want a water ice to cool you off?"

"Lemon-flavored, please," Margaret said with a smile as she watched Dave venture over to the water ice vendor. She knew he'd order a cherry-flavored for himself, though lemon was usually her go-to flavor.

"Alright! The votes are in!" the official announced. "We're going to start with third place ... which goes to the Johnson sisters. They did the beach chair sand sculpture. Everyone, give them a round of applause!"

Margaret and Dave clapped, while looking around the beach. They hadn't even seen that one.

"OK, second place. That goes to Mark Everly! He did the mermaid. Congrats Mark," the woman yelled as everyone clapped on the beach. "Now, let's have a drumroll for the first-place winner. This is for the thousand-dollar prize. And our winner is ... Wally Dunk for the blue whale!"

Wally stood next to his whale and waved to everyone on the beach while taking a bow.

The woman got back on the megaphone. "This is Wally's third win this year so far. He's got talent. That's for sure!"

Dave took a bite of his cherry water ice, which stained his lips red in the process. "Would you look at that. Good for Wally. I know talent when I see it."

Margaret chuckled and rolled her eyes. "Well, *talent* is all around you out here, but yes, Wally has got a lot of it," she said as she savored a spoonful of her cold citrus water ice.

Dave finished his, then looked at Margaret as she ate her last spoonful. "Wanna take the long way back to the car? I feel like going for a stroll."

Margaret wiped some sweat off her brow with the back of her arm. "Sounds good to me as long as we pick streets shaded by some trees."

Dave began walking but stopped when his empty stomach started growling. "I don't think that water ice filled me up much. Why don't we swing by Hot Dog Tommy's first? It is lunchtime, after all," he said, glancing at his watch.

Margaret playfully nudged Dave. "Oh, I knew you were going to work in getting Hot Dog Tommy's today. I *knew* it! You've been talking about going there for months."

Dave shrugged. "What can I say. I've been craving a good hot dog since baseball season started."

They held hands as they walked along the promenade

towards Jackson Street. Margaret took a deep breath as she looked back towards the ocean.

"What's on your mind?" Dave asked.

Margaret let out a sigh. "I was just thinking how the girls would have loved the sand sculpting contest. I wish they were here with us to see it."

Dave squeezed Margaret's hand. "We'll bring them next year. Paul has them for a fun long weekend that they were very excited about."

Margaret smiled as they approached Jackson Street and crossed Beach Avenue. "You're right. Plus, I know Paul was looking forward to taking the girls on a little adventure in Lancaster. He even got permission to pull them out of school a day early. They're probably on their way now."

As they crossed the street, Dave's eyes widened when he saw the long line outside of Hot Dog Tommy's. "Looks like everyone in town is craving a hot dog too."

Margaret led Dave to the end of the line by his hand, and before they knew it, they were at the eatery's window giving their order.

Dave looked over the extensive hot dog menu as Margaret ordered. "I think I'll have the Slaw Dog."

"What's on that?" Dave asked as he squinted, trying to find it on the menu.

Margaret pointed. "It's right there. Hot dog with yellow mustard and Miss Mary's coleslaw."

Dave nodded. "Sounds great, but I think I'm going to go with the Shaggy Dog. It's a hot dog with shredded cheddar cheese and sauerkraut."

They received their hot dogs, then stood off to the side, eating them while looking back at the line.

Dave rolled his eyes back in his head and groaned as he took a bite and chewed. "You've got to be kidding me. This is incredible."

Margaret chuckled as she finished her bite and swallowed. "It definitely hit the spot. You about ready to stroll?"

Dave nodded as he finished the last of the hot dog. "You bet," he said as he put his arm around Margaret's waist and started walking.

Margaret sighed as she looked at the gorgeous homes that lined the street before stopping in front of a bright-yellow Victorian house with a huge front porch and a black wrought iron fence around the yard. "Sometimes I daydream about what it would be like to live in one of these."

Dave leaned on the fence and looked the house over. "It would be something, wouldn't it? Though, the Seahorse Inn is just as majestic, no?"

Margaret nodded in thought. "It is ... in its own way, but it's a bed-and-breakfast. This is a whole house ... a private residence that you don't have to share with other guests, just your loved ones."

Dave rubbed his chin as he eyed the bright-blue gingerbread trim then the trendy rustic furniture on the porch, when he suddenly noticed people sitting in the chairs looking back at them. "Oh, jeez. This is awkward. I think these people think we've been staring at them this whole time."

"Who?" Margaret asked as she squinted her eyes.

Before Dave could answer, a woman in one of the chairs stood up and walked towards the porch railing, looking at them the entire time.

"Sorry, we were just looking!" Dave yelled over with a chuckle as he took Margaret's hand, signaling they should keep it moving.

"Wait!" the woman yelled back.

Dave and Margaret turned around, only a few steps away from where they just had been.

"Is that ... Dave? Dave Patterson?" the woman said while shielding the sun from her eyes with her hand.

Dave widened his eyes as he and Margaret headed back to the wrought iron fence. "It is. Do I know you?"

The woman clapped her hands excitedly before turning around to her husband, who was sitting on the porch with his feet up on an ottoman and eyes closed. "I told you it was him."

The man opened one eye. "Who?"

The woman waved her husband off, then looked back at Dave. "Do you know who I am?"

Dave shook his head, then glanced back at Margaret and shrugged his shoulders. "I'm sorry, but I don't."

"It's Heather."

Dave scratched his head while Margaret chuckled, getting a kick out of the whole conversation.

Dave stared at Heather until a light bulb went off. "Wait. Heather? Heather from high school? Heather Scarpo? The Heather that would beat all the guys at soccer after school? The one whose dad let us have big bonfires out on the family property? That's you?"

Heather laughed as her husband got up and stood beside her to see what was going on. "Yes. This is my husband, Troy," she said motioning to him. "I tell him all the time about those good ol' days. We had fun, didn't we?"

Troy nodded. "She does. Apparently, my high school experience pales in comparison. She makes it sound like it was something out of a TV show."

Dave laughed as he put his arm around Margaret's shoulders. "This is my wife, Margaret."

Margaret waved and smiled. "Nice to meet you two. Love your home! I hope you didn't think we were creeps staring at it for as long as we did."

Heather waved her hand. "Oh, we're used to it. Are you guys busy? Would you two like to come hang out and have some wine and cheese?"

Without even asking Dave, Margaret spoke up. "We'd love to!"

Dave opened the gate latch, and they walked up the steps to the dreamy, shaded porch where a bottle of red wine and a plate of cheese and crackers sat.

Heather hugged Dave and Margaret, while Troy shook their hands.

"Take a seat, and I'll go grab some extra wineglasses," Troy said as he headed inside.

Margaret sat next to Dave on a love seat and looked the porch up and down in amazement before her eyes landed on the street. Suddenly, they were on the other side of the fence watching all the passersby stop to look at the gorgeous Victorian. It almost felt like they were royalty.

"So, this is your place?" Dave asked just as Troy came back outside with two wineglasses.

Heather nodded as Troy took his seat next to her, then proceeded to pour the wine for Dave and Margaret. "It is. All those years of medical school paid off," she said with a chuckle.

Troy cut in. "She means med school for both of us. We're both doctors. I'm a cardiologist and she's a gastroenterologist."

Heather handed the glasses of wine to Dave and Margaret. "We're also good with investments, like this place. It's our summer home, but we like to rent it out most of the time."

Dave took a sip of the cabernet. "Oh yeah? What's the weekly going rate for a place like this?"

Troy tapped his fingers on the arm of the chair. "About twenty thousand."

Margaret almost choked on her wine. "Wow! For a week?"

Heather shrugged. "It's a lot, I know, but people pay it. It's a seven-bedroom house, so we usually get large families, and I'm assuming they all divide the cost between themselves. Plus, it's right in the thick of Cape May, walking distance to the Washington Street Mall, the beach, and the restaurants."

Dave popped a piece of cheese into his mouth. "I'll say. It's gorgeous."

Heather leaned back into her chair. "So, what's new? I

haven't spoken to you, Dave, since graduation. Can you believe that was almost thirty years ago?"

Dave took a long sigh, then grabbed Margaret's hand. "I'll keep it short. Life really started to get good three years ago when Margaret and I started dating. We both worked at Pinetree Wildlife Refuge and met at just the right time. We fell in love, got married, started new businesses, bought a beach house on the bay in North Cape May that is now a rental property, and last year we bought a farmhouse on a huge plot of land out in West Cape May. We have two daughters, Margaret's from her first marriage, but I now consider them mine as well. They're with their father today, so we decided to enjoy the day in Cape May."

A dreamy look appeared in Heather's eyes. "A farmhouse? In West Cape May? Are you serious?"

Troy chuckled as he sipped his wine. "Heather wanted a farmhouse in West Cape May more than this house when we were looking for properties. This one seemed the better investment for rentals."

Heather sighed and shook her head. "He's right. I still think about it. Maybe someday. We live in Maine but try to get down here when we can. Usually, a week here or there."

Margaret smiled. "We love our farmhouse. It's beautiful in every way, but these huge Victorians have their own unique beauty too."

Heather abruptly stood up. "How silly of me! Did you guys want a tour of the place?"

Margaret's eyes widened as she squeezed Dave's arm. "We'd love that. You have time?"

"Yes, totally," Heather said as she walked towards the front door.

Troy stood with his glass of wine and rolled his eyes while laughing. "She does this with everybody that visits. Barely lets them get a word in before she's showing every room in the house."

"Don't listen to him," Heather said jokingly as Dave and Margaret followed her inside.

They'd barely made it to the primary bedroom upstairs when Troy came inside calling for Heather. "Hon. Where are you?"

"We're up here!" Heather yelled.

Troy went up the stairs, holding his phone, to find them all in the hallway. "I've got bad news, dear."

Heather gasped and held her heart. "What?"

Troy shook his head. "No, not like that. Nothing serious."

Heather breathed a sigh of relief. "Then, don't come up here saying stuff like that. Are you trying to give me a heart attack? You're a cardiologist. You should know better."

Troy sighed. "Work just called. There's an emergency and they need me. My fill-in just came down with an illness, so I've got to get back up to Maine."

Heather felt the blood drain from her face. She'd been so excited to spend Memorial Day weekend at their home in Cape May. It had been months since they'd had any free time to even get to the Jersey Shore. "You're kidding. When do you need to be there?"

"Tomorrow morning, ideally."

Margaret and Dave showed themselves to the primary bedroom for their own tour so as to not awkwardly stand there during the couple's conversation.

Troy walked over to Heather and rubbed her arms. "Look, normally this wouldn't happen since Dr. Groff was filling in for me, but he, apparently, has been sick for days and has been bedridden. I start my new job—remember, that's a Monday through Friday only thing—next month. We won't have to deal with this then, I promise."

Heather sighed. "I know .... Well, I'll start packing. Guess we need to leave ASAP. I wish I'd known. We could have rented this place out all weekend."

Troy nodded. "I'll try and drive most of the way."

Margaret and Dave walked back out into the hallway awkwardly, after hearing their conversation end.

"Well, it's a lovely place you have," Margaret said, breaking the silence.

Heather looked over at Troy and back at Margaret and Dave. "Would you two like to stay here for Memorial Day weekend? Free of charge? We'd really like someone to enjoy this place. The weather is going to be perfect."

Troy cleared his throat. "If you have responsible friends and family, you can invite them too. Enjoy the holiday weekend. Heck, stay the week. You just have to be out by Saturday morning as our cleaning service comes around 11a.m. to prepare the house for our next weekly rental."

Dave's eyes widened. "Wow. Thank you for the offer but —"

Margaret cut him off. "But we'd love to. We're already off until Monday. We can stop in at home to check on things, and my daughters are with their dad until Tuesday. We'd love to invite our close friends and some family if that would be OK, though not sure who can make it on such short notice."

Dave looked at Margaret with surprise. "Really?"

Before Margaret could respond, Troy cut in. "That's wonderful. We'll show you everything you need to know, and you can leave the keys in the mail slot when you leave. Our cleaning service has their own keys."

Heather smiled. "Well, I'm glad *someone* gets to enjoy this place if we can't. The downside to our careers is sometimes having to be on-call, but it looks like that will change next month."

Dave shook hands with Troy while Margaret hugged Heather. "We can't thank you enough for this generous offer."

Suddenly, two kids came running up the steps completely covered in mud. "Mom! Dad! The Slip 'N Slide in the backyard is covered in mud."

Heather held her hands to her mouth. "You two, get

11

outside *now*. You're getting mud everywhere. I'm hosing you off before your showers." The kids ran back downstairs towards the yard while Heather shook her head and laughed. "You're going to love it here. Trust me. The only payback we need is to invite us to your farmhouse so I can live that dream a little."

Margaret smiled as she looked around the gorgeous old home. "We'd love to show you our place the next time you're in town, and I've actually got a great idea for how to spend our weekend here."

CHAPTER TWO

"You've got to be *kidding* me," Donna said as she stepped through the front door of the gorgeous Victorian, eyeing the tall built-in bookcases full of old leather-bound books and vintage nautical decor. "*This* is where we're staying?"

Dale followed behind her, stopping in his tracks to stare at the huge chandelier in the foyer. It stole the attention from everything else in the room. "It all feels perfectly preserved here."

Dave lugged two suitcases through the door, his and Margaret's, and set them by the solid wood banister before glancing up the staircase. "Twenty thousand a week. That's the going rate for this place."

Dale's eyes widened. "I believe it. Having a place like this to ourselves, feels like something out of a movie."

Suddenly, voices could be heard outside getting closer, then Margaret, Sarah, Chris, Liz, and Greg stepped inside.

Margaret walked towards Dave with pep in her step, then spun around to face everyone and leaned her arm on the banister, feeling quite proud. "Well, this is it, guys! I can't believe we pulled this off with less than twenty-four hours' notice."

Liz shook her head and laughed. "I can't either. It just so happened that Greg's parents were able to come stay at our house and watch the boys and dogs."

Sarah smiled and glanced up at Chris. "And I have some pretty great employees at the Book Nook, wouldn't you say?"

Chris nodded. "You do. They're great. Now, as far as my new employees running the Blue Heron Birding Boat this weekend? I'll get back to you and let you know," he said with a slight chuckle.

Margaret nodded, then glanced around the room at everyone. "Dave's friend graciously allowed us to stay here free of charge. They usually rent it out, however, this week they had planned to be here, but something had come up with work in Maine. I couldn't be more thankful to them for this opportunity. OK, well, how about I'll give everyone a quick tour, then we'll pick our rooms. Follow me," she said as she walked towards the kitchen.

A knock came at the front door, and they stopped in their tracks, everyone turning around.

"Are we expecting someone else?" Chris half-joked.

Donna threw her hand up to her mouth and gasped. "Oh my gosh! Lisa! I forgot I invited her," she said as she threw the door open to a forty-six-year-old woman with long dirty-blonde hair wearing a cropped tank top and jean shorts.

"Donna!" Lisa squealed as she wrapped her arms around her friend for a big hug.

"I can't believe you were able to make it. What happened? I never heard back from you yesterday," Donna asked while everyone stood by and watched.

"You know, I wasn't completely sure if I was going to be back in Cape May in time, but the stars aligned," Lisa said with a smile.

Donna laughed. "Well, I'm so glad it worked out. Did you need help bringing your stuff in?"

Lisa pointed to the street where a lime-green Volkswagen

Bus sat with two surfboards mounted to the roof. "Oh, I've only got a small duffel bag. You know what they say … travel light, travel far."

Donna gasped. "How rude of me. I haven't introduced you to my friends," she said as she turned around to face everyone and put her arm around Lisa's shoulders.

The gang smiled and waved somewhat awkwardly, still not sure of who this new person was, though Margaret remembered Donna had mentioned the possibility of her friend coming.

"This is my old friend Lisa. We played softball together in college. When we found out we both had ties to Cape May, we became best buds," Donna said turning to Lisa.

"Then, you stayed in California, and I moved to Hawaii, and now we're here in Cape May … together," Lisa said with a smile.

Donna nodded. "She called me yesterday, and we caught up for hours."

"Then, I mentioned I was looking to spend the summer in Cape May but wasn't sure when I'd get here. There's only so much mileage I can put on ol' Gertie over there," Lisa said while pointing to her VW Bus.

Sarah reached her hand out first. "Great to meet you, Lisa. I'm Sarah, and that's my fiancé Chris."

Lisa shook Sarah's hand as Margaret and Dave introduced themselves, followed by Liz and Greg.

Donna walked over to Dale and planted a kiss on his cheek. "And last but not least is my fiancé, Dale. The one I talked all about yesterday."

Dale chuckled. "I hope it was all *amazing* things."

Lisa smiled as she gave Dale a hug, then whispered in his ear, "You got a good one, Dale."

Dale smiled and felt his face flush as he stepped back from the embrace. "It's great to finally meet you, Lisa. Heard all wonderful things."

Margaret let out a happy sigh as the conversation died down. "You got here just in time, Lisa, I was about to give the official tour of the place before we pick our rooms. Follow me into the kitchen."

Moments later, they all stood in the ornate kitchen. Its many windows helped an overall dark room stand out by allowing natural light to stream in. All the cabinets were black with gold pulls, the flooring was black-and-white tile, and two large chandeliers hung over a kitchen island. It had definitely been remodeled but still had a Victorian flair.

"So, the kitchen and the bathrooms are the most modern out of the entire house. It's gorgeous, isn't it?" Margaret said she turned around to peek at the fresh bouquets of flowers that Heather had put out on the countertops.

Everyone nodded excitedly as they eyed the entire room, finding new and interesting things everywhere they looked.

"Breathtaking," Liz said as she studied a small stained-glass window above the fridge.

Greg nodded. "That's saying a lot coming from my wife, the interior designer."

Liz playfully pinched Greg's side, feeling a tinge of embarrassment.

Dave headed out into the living room where a large fireplace sat bordered by floor-to-ceiling bookshelves and boasted another chandelier. "Here's the living room. It's got some pretty comfy-looking couches, too," he said as he flopped down in one.

Dale and Chris sat down on the couch on either side of Dave, while Greg plopped into a chair, and they all kicked their feet up onto the large ottoman. "We'll be here while you all tour the rest of the house," Dale joked.

Margaret, who was showing the ladies the dining room, then looked over at the guys. "OK, that's fine, but that means we'll be picking out the rooms, then."

The guys immediately popped up off the couch and rushed

up the staircase. "I'm guessing these Victorians probably don't have king beds in the them, huh?" Chris asked.

Dave laughed. "It may be queens for us all weekend, but here's hoping."

Dale shook his head. "Anything is better than a double bed. We once accidentally booked a room at a B&B with a double bed. For two people that like their space while sleeping, it was, well … let's just say I hung off the edge of the bed all night. It's a miracle I didn't roll off."

The ladies appeared in the upstairs hallway as the guys each picked their favorite room, took their shoes off, and laid on the bed to make sure it suited them.

Margaret laughed as she listened to the men banter back and forth between rooms.

"I sleep in. None of you better be loud snorers," Chris said while laughing.

Dale shook his head. "I don't snore, but I do sleepwalk. Better lock your door if you don't want any surprises," he joked.

Dave laughed from the room he was in. "Yeah … well I sleepwalk too. Maybe Dale and I will go on some night adventures in this ol' home together."

Margaret chuckled. "If you sleepwalk, I was not made aware of it." She turned to Lisa and pointed to the only room left on the second floor. "Guess that's your room. Does that work?"

Lisa's eyes widened as she glanced inside the beautifully decorated room full of vases of dried hydrangeas and lace curtains, then to the large Victorian-style canopy bed. "This is absolutely perfect."

Liz looked at the ladies. "How about the guys bring the luggage up, and then we can get started with planning out the rest of the day?"

Greg hopped off the bed. "I'm on it, dear," he said as he stuck his head into the rooms that Dale and Dave were in.

"Hey, guys. Get up! We're being ordered to bring the luggage inside."

* * *

Judy drove along Route 95 South while Bob opened a large old map, completely obscuring his face from view. "It appears we're looking for Route 1, then Route 13," he said as he ran his finger over the map.

Judy shook her head. "Bob, this is ridiculous. We have a built-in GPS on our phones now. Let's use that."

Bob lowered the map to look at Judy. "Like I said, I miss the old days of using actual paper maps. It's exciting and enlightening. I'd study all the nearby roads and towns. You don't really see the big picture on the GPS," he said while opening the map back up wide enough to almost cover the dashboard.

Judy sighed and chuckled. "Well, you're definitely getting the *big* picture there."

Bob took his left hand off the map and pushed his glasses up the bridge of his nose and looked over at Judy. "I'm surprised we even need directions. We've been to the Outer Banks before."

Judy shrugged. "Bob, that was fifteen years ago for my cousin Marty when he married Lois. We need the directions."

Bob nodded and chuckled. "You're right," he said as he folded the map up and set it in his lap. "Now, we're headed down for Cousin Marty's second marriage to Jane."

Judy tried not to laugh at Bob's comment while attempting to glare at him. "Well, Lois wasn't a good match for him, I guess. Jane seems nice, though."

Bob shook his head. "What are you talking about? We haven't even met her yet."

"Oh, you know … just from hearing about her. Linda had

18

lunch with her and Marty a few weeks ago," Judy said as she stared at the road.

"Mike's coming, right?" Bob asked.

Judy nodded. "Yes, Linda and Mike will be there. Carol, Jack, Debbie, Phil, the whole family … plus Jane's side."

"And this house is big enough for us, your brothers and sisters, and everyone else?" Bob asked, starting to feel skeptical about the holiday weekend.

Judy sighed, remembering they had already discussed this a week ago. "Yes. It's a huge house in Duck, North Carolina right on the beach. Twelve bedrooms, each with their own bathroom. There's even an elevator."

"Oh, that's right. I do remember you talking about this now," Bob said while pulling his phone out of his pocket and hitting some buttons on the screen.

Judy glanced over. "Pull up the house listing to see how gorgeous this place is."

Bob swiped his screen until he came to Judy's email. *Just My Duck* was the name of the house in the listing. All of the houses in Duck had neat names on the front, a lot of times pertaining to the town's name. He magnified the first picture of the house with his fingers, which showed an aqua colored mansion with a beachfront view and decks galore. It appeared almost every room had a deck attached to it. He swiped to the first picture, which revealed the kitchen with two ovens, two stoves, two dishwashers, and yep, two refrigerators. Next to the kitchen was a table long enough to fit twenty-five people, and past that, was the living room with two wraparound couches and ceiling-high windows that led to a deck overlooking the beach, the perfect spot to catch the East Coast sunrise.

"Well, what do you think?" Judy asked, after noticing Bob had been quite silent while staring at the photos.

Bob chuckled. "It's … pretty impressive. I'll say that."

Judy smirked, feeling proud of herself, even though she didn't have any part in booking in the place. *Her* family did have good taste in houses, after all, though. "Keep going. Wait until you see the first floor," Judy said while turning the radio up a little.

Bob swiped again until he came to a theater room, complete with twenty recliners on tiered flooring so every seat had a good view of the large screen. He swiped again to see the bedrooms, many of which were fitted with king beds and their own TVs. Then he saw the game room, which had a pool table and another TV with a wraparound couch. He rubbed his eyes and set his phone down. "Well, the place looks great. I'm looking forward to getting there," he said as he glanced at his watch, noticing they had another five hours of driving.

Judy turned the radio down again. "Did you see the photos of the pool area?"

Bob shook his head. "I stopped at the game room. I started feeling carsick from looking at my phone."

Judy sighed happily as she merged onto Route 13. "Well, it's a huge heated pool with a waterfall, then there're two hot tubs by the pool and two more on the decks. The pool also has a neat tiki bar with stools and plenty of lounge chairs to relax in. Not to mention, right outside of the pool's fencing is our personal path straight to the beach. It's going to be pure bliss."

Bob put his hand on Judy's shoulder. "Like I said, this place looks and sounds impressive. I'm sure it'll be wonderful," he said while turning to glance at the back seat. "By the way, what all did you make?"

Judy looked in the rearview mirror at the cooler and box full of casserole dishes and a crock pot. "Well, we're doing potlucks this weekend. I've decided to go with an Italian feast. I made two lasagnas. Mike, Linda, Debbie, Jack and Carol are in charge of the meatballs, sausage, garlic bread, and salad. For dessert, Phil's making cannoli. Not sure what everyone else at the house will be making."

Bob felt his belly rumble hearing about all the delicious food, then yawned, leaned his head back, and started to drift off. "Just let me know what you need me to do, hon. I can drive whenever you're ready to take a break," he said as he fell into a deep sleep.

Judy smiled, then glanced down, noticing the map that had been on Bob's lap had fallen by his feet. She turned her GPS on, and started her newest audiobook, then breathed a sigh of relief as she got comfy and ready for the long drive ahead.

CHAPTER THREE

By early Saturday afternoon, the Cape May Victorian house was abuzz with the group of friends, ready to start their exciting weekend. Sarah leaned over the kitchen island, munching on crudités while Donna sipped her wine.

"So, you don't want a bachelorette party? That's what you're saying?" Sarah said as she popped a carrot stick in her mouth.

Donna grabbed a slice of cucumber and took a bite, then washed it down with a sip of rose wine. "Yes. Well, at least not in the traditional sense. I don't want shirts that say Bride Tribe. I don't want any sashes to wear, and I *certainly* don't want any of those gaudy cheesy decorations and straws and what not. I mean, really, I don't *need* one."

Sarah looked around the room. "Well, maybe we can come up with something that suits you. Something you'd actually enjoy."

Donna nodded. "I guess, but I don't want a spectacle made. Plus, what about you and Chris?"

Sarah chuckled and looked over her shoulder to make sure nobody was listening. "Well, we don't have a clue when or where we're getting married yet. I thought I'd be in a rush, but

I'm not. I want to take our time and find the perfect location, you know?"

Donna smiled while taking another gulp of wine. "I said the same thing. Then, bam! I was ready to get married. Maybe it was all those romantic comedy movies I watched that weekend, but I'm so ready for a wedding with the *right* man this time."

"I get it. I really do. You and Dale both get to have your marriage done right this time around, whereas this is Chris's second wedding but my first. That part feels a little *weird* to me," Sarah said, slightly ashamed.

"Why?" Donna asked.

"Well, he's been down this road. I never have. I'll probably want all those traditional things you see at a wedding—the bouquet toss, the dances with the parents, the garter, the white dress, the emotions and jitters of finally saying 'I do' to that one person in the world you want to spend your life with. I've never done all that, and he *did*. I just get a feeling that since this is his second marriage, he probably wants something simple," Sarah finished as the rest of group filed into the kitchen.

Margaret walked up to them and reached over to grab a bright-yellow bell pepper strip. She took a bite, looked around the room at everyone, and said, "OK, the plan today is to head over to Wildwood Boardwalk to walk the boards and see Donna and Dale's new funnel cake *storefront*."

Everyone turned their attention to Dale and Donna and clapped.

"Thank you. Thank you," Donna said while smiling at Dale. "As you know, the funnel cake stand had its best year yet last summer, and we were more than ready to get a larger space, and one just happened to open up in the perfect spot."

Dale looked at Donna, beaming with pride. "Donna quadrupled the funnel cake business earnings since she took it over. I may have to hire you for the restaurant, dear," he said half-jokingly.

Donna shrugged. "I don't know. I'm quite enjoying this funnel cake venture."

Everyone smiled at their exchange as Margaret cleared her throat. "OK, now back to today …. We'll head back here to wash up and change after Wildwood, then grab dinner at a new little oyster bar right on the bay I just discovered, then—"

Liz interrupted. "Wait a minute. I heard about that oyster place. Where they harvest the oysters is not too far away."

Greg nodded. "Supposed to be some great oysters. It's called Joe's Oyster Bar. I've already contacted them about getting some oysters for my restaurant."

Dale glanced at Greg. "Mind if I do the same?"

Greg smiled. "Definitely not. No need to ask."

Margaret grabbed her keys off the counter. "Who's driving besides us? We need one more car to get to Wildwood."

Lisa raised her hand. "Anyone feel like taking a spin in Gertie? She's lots of fun to drive in."

"I'm in!" Sarah said as she grabbed her purse from the chair and followed everyone outside to the cars.

* * *

Walking on the Wildwood Boardwalk, the midday sun had come out in full force, as did the crowds for the holiday weekend.

"We're about halfway down," Donna said as they rubber-necked the happenings around them.

On the group's right, a monster truck had constructed a track in the sand on a long stretch of beach where people paid to get rides. Some mounds of sand along the course were for the truck to drive over, which the participants, who sat in the open-air back of the truck, seemed to enjoy.

Then, there were the roller coasters and all of those spin rides that seemed to make you feel sicker the older you got.

Dave interlocked his fingers with Margaret's, then pointed

with his other hand to one of the many stores full of neon-colored clothing with *Wildwood* emblazoned on them.

Lisa chuckled. "Some things never change. Wildwood is still Wildwood after all these years."

Sarah squinted her eyes to read a sign from a store that had loud pulsating dance music reverberating onto the boardwalk. "World's best ... pizza ...."

Chris chuckled. "Well, would you look at that! World's best, right here in Wildwood."

Sarah shrugged. "It actually looks quite good. We'll have to try it someday and give our review."

Just then, the sea of people walking ahead of their group parted, and "Watch the tramcar, please" sounded from the speakers of the bright-yellow tramcar full of people hitching a ride down the long two-and-a-half-mile boardwalk.

"Everyone, out of the way," Dave alerted, so they all stepped aside to let the tramcar pass.

Donna sighed happily as she turned to watch, then looked back at the group. "Can you believe the tramcar has been running since 1949? It's incredible, isn't it?"

Liz nodded. "I believe it. Two-plus miles of walking on this hot boardwalk, especially after a long day of rides with kids, can do you in."

They'd continued on and were walking through crowds when a young man running a game booth pointed to them. "Step right up! Can you get the frog onto the moving lily pad?"

Dale's eyes widened. "Oh, I've gotta play. I loved this game growing up," he said, walking over to the guy. He handed the man some money for him and Donna.

Dave paid for Margaret and himself, then all four were handed long green rubber frogs and a mallet while the rest of the group stood back and watched.

"How do I do this?" Margaret asked.

Dave stood behind her and took one of her frogs, folded it, and put it in the launching device. "See this red knob here, you

25

hit that with a mallet, and it launches your frog toward the moving lily pads. Object is to get one to 'hop' on."

"Oh, OK," Margaret said as she smashed the mallet down. To her utter surprise, the frog landed square on the lily pad.

Dave's eyes widened in amazement as he got his frog ready for launch. "You got one on!"

"Oh my gosh, I did!" Margaret squealed as she watched the frog spin on the lily pad.

Two more rounds later, Margaret had won three stuffed animals that she promptly gave away to kids on the boardwalk, and Donna had won two, leaving the guys bewildered that they came away empty-handed but proud of their ladies at the same time.

"I love that game. Wasn't that great?" Margaret asked Donna.

Donna nodded as they walked down the boardwalk. "We killed it! You and I could be a team, Marg. I think we could do big things."

Margaret laughed. "Or win *big* stuffed animals."

Sarah stopped in her tracks as she searched for the *clanks* and *whooshes* that could only come from a wooden roller coaster.

"There's the Great White. Probably one of the few roller coasters I'll go on since it doesn't go upside down," Chris said as he stopped and stared with Sarah.

"What are you guys looking at?" Greg asked as he walked up beside them.

Sarah pointed to the wooden tracks off in the distance. "Anyone want to go on?"

Surprisingly, everyone nodded. "I'm game," Dave said before approaching the ticket stand. Then everyone handed him money for their tickets too.

Soon they were in line for the roller coaster, and before they knew it, they were up at the front and boarding. Each couple sat together, and Lisa got seated next to a thirteen-year-old boy who had alerted her that this was his fifth time in a row going on this ride.

"Here we go!" Margaret yelled as she put her arms up in the air and the vehicle took off on the track.

First it went up a big incline, then sped down, making their stomachs jump into their throats while at the same time giving them the biggest thrill, till finally they were at the end and deboarding.

Dale held his back as they walked to the exit of the ride.

"You alright, old man?" Dave joked as he put his hand on Dale's shoulder.

Dale chuckled. "I think all that jostling around up there got me good. No one ever warns you about that part of getting older. The wrinkles? Yes. The grays? Yes. The balding? Yes. An injury from riding a roller coasters? Nope."

Everyone laughed while Donna turned a little green. "I think my stomach is still up there somewhere," she said feeling a tinge of nausea set in.

Dale put his other arm around Donna's shoulders. "We can be hurt and sick together, dear," he said while nuzzling his face in her cheek.

Donna laughed. "We're fine. A trip to the chiropractor and the drugstore will fix us right up."

As they headed back towards the boardwalk, the crowds had grown even thicker. Tons of people walked around in bathing suits and flip-flops, coming right from the beach, looking for a bite to eat before hopping back in the ocean.

Donna shielded her eyes from the sun and looked past the crowds. "It's a little further down."

Lisa stopped in the middle of the boardwalk and gasped with pleasure. "The Original Old Time Photo is still here? You've got to be kidding me. My family took one of these photos every year, framed them, and hung them on the wall. I can't believe it."

Everyone nodded and chuckled as they walked towards the

photography studio to look at the Wild West-type costumes and props that you could dress up in for your posed vintage-style photographs in front of a saloon set. Almost all of them had a photo done at one point in their life.

"Let's do one … for nostalgia's sake," Margaret said with excitement and widened eyes. "I'll buy."

"OK," Sarah said and headed in, followed by everyone else.

Margaret paid, and they went over and picked their costumes, hats, gloves, and props, and changed into them. While waiting to be posed in front of the saloon, the group waited on Dave, who was taking a lot longer getting ready.

"You alright in the there?" Margaret asked.

"I'm OK," Dave said from behind the dressing room curtain, "I just feel … a little silly."

Greg laughed. "We all do. That's the fun of it. Get on out here."

The curtain was pushed to the side, and out came Dave in a western hat with his salt-and-pepper hair peeking out from under the brim, a bandana around his neck, and wearing a long brown coat. The outfit seemed to fit his rustic surfer-lumberjack style perfectly.

Margaret felt her heart leap out of her chest as she stared at him with starry eyes. "Wow. I *love* that on you. It looks great."

Dave brushed some dust off his sleeve. "You think?"

Margaret smiled. "Oh, I know. It looks incredible. I think you would have fit right in with that style back then."

"OK, everyone. They're ready for us," Sarah said as one of the workers positioned her on a stool.

Next thing they knew, all nine of them were either standing or sitting on stools and smiling for the camera. By the time they left, Donna was even more eager to get to the funnel cake stand, and the rest of the group was too—they were ready for the reveal of its name, which Donna and Dale had been quite mum about.

"There it is," Dale said, pointing.

Sure enough, right between a pizza and hot dog stand, there stood Dale and Donna's Funnel Cakes. Everyone took notice of the store name and gasped.

"Dale and Donna's?" Dave said as he stared.

Dale shook his head and chuckled. "Donna insisted. I named my restaurant after her, so she felt that the funnel cake stand should be both of our names."

"Oh, I love that," Sarah said, feeling her heart burst.

Donna nodded. "Yep, I got my way. Dale and Donna's has a nice ring to it anyway. Dale started the funnel cake stand, and I took over. I think both names should be part of it. Come see the inside. I absolutely love the way it came out," she said leading them towards the counter and around a line that had formed on the boardwalk.

"Hi, Derck!" Donna said as she waved to the cashier.

"Hey, Donna," Derek said, surprised to see her.

"I know I said I wasn't going to be here, but I had to show my friends the place," Donna said, pointing to the group.

They all followed Donna to the back of the store where the tables for eating were. Since every seat was occupied, they crammed into a corner and looked around.

"This is wonderful. Look how busy it is," Margaret said, noticing the piping-hot, delicious funnel cakes on every table.

Dale put his arm around Donna. "This is Donna's baby, and she's doing a fantastic job. Look at the way this place is running ... it's like a well-oiled machine."

Donna nodded. "That's because I provide top-notch training to my employees. Having good employees is worth its weight in gold."

Dale noticed there was less and less room for them to stand in the corner anymore. "Anyone ready to get some food? I know a great sit-down pizza place that also has salads and sandwiches."

"The real question is … is there air-conditioning?" Liz asked, feeling herself start to sweat.

"There definitely is," Dale said as he led the group back out onto the boardwalk.

Margaret and Dave followed in the rear, holding hands and feeling like two teenagers again. The afternoon on the board-walk couldn't have been any more perfect.

CHAPTER FOUR

After lunch at the Wildwood Boardwalk, they went back to the Victorian to shower, change, and relax before the evening festivities.

Dave rummaged through the fridge. "You said this was a BYOB, Margaret?"

"Yes, we've got some wine and beer we can bring," Margaret said as she stepped onto the back deck with the rest of the gang.

"I see it," Dave said as he filled the small cooler next to him with ice.

Outside, the yard seemed to be a whole other exciting wing of the house that hadn't yet been explored.

Greg walked over to the large pizza oven sitting atop a small brick patio in the corner of the yard. "Liz, I found my birthday gift."

Liz walked up next to him. "Wow, an outdoor pizza oven. I haven't seen one of these in years. Where would we even put it?"

Greg shrugged. "I really don't know," he said turning to the group who had dispersed to different areas. "Anyone down for homemade pizzas this weekend?"

"Oh, definitely, yes," Lisa said as she came over to inspect the oven.

Everyone else answered affirmatively while scoping out the lush, thick grass, the fire pit, and the many solar lights tucked away within the pristinely landscaped yard.

Margaret looked at her watch. "We'd better get going. I have it timed that we have an hour or so to walk around and see the oyster farm, then we should be eating or done eating by the time the sun is setting over the bay."

Donna chuckled. "You are the perfect planner. Want to plan my wedding?"

Sarah cleared her throat. "Donna, your wedding is July 4. I *hope* it's planned by now."

Donna laughed awkwardly. "Well, for the most part, it's all set to go. Just have to iron out a few more details, but that will be easy."

Margaret breathed a sigh of relief. "Glad to hear that. Our property is ready for the big event. Just let us know what we can do."

Lisa walked up next to them. "Did I overhear that correctly? The wedding is on Margaret and Dave's property?"

Donna nodded. "Yes, it is. Their property is exquisite. Wait until you see it. I feel so lucky to have these amazing friends."

Dave stood on the patio with the cooler by his side. "You guys ready? Time to pile in the vehicles again."

"Perfect. We can drive this time," Chris said as he followed Dave through the house.

"Us too," Greg said while everyone followed behind him towards the cars.

* * *

By five o'clock, it had hit low tide on the Delaware Bay—perfect timing to see the oyster farm. They stood by and watched as a handful of men, dressed in waders, sorted oysters on tables.

"Look at that. Seems like they're sorting the oysters by size," Dave said feeling quite interested in the entire process.

Liz found herself distracted by some fish that jumped around in the water and pointed them out to Greg while Sarah and Chris found a dry spot of sand to sit and watch the action quietly.

Donna nudged Lisa, noticing she hadn't taken her eyes off the oyster crewmen. "Big oyster fan?"

Lisa turned to Donna. "Actually, yes. Love them," she said before casting her eyes back towards the workers.

Donna followed Lisa's gaze to a six-foot-four crewman with thick blond hair and crystal-blue eyes glancing at Lisa and slipping a quick smile.

Lisa diverted her eyes. "I'm going to head inside and find the bathroom," she said walking quickly across the driveway.

Donna shrugged, then got Margaret's attention. "Should we go in and get our table?"

Margaret looked at her watch. "Yes, we're a little early, but I'm starving. I say we go get sat,"

They walked across the gravel driveway to the host stand where Lisa also met back up with them.

"Hi. We have a party of nine under Margaret," Margaret said to the host, feeling proud of herself that she managed to even get a reservation. Joe's Oyster Bar seemed harder than ever to get into for dinner lately.

The host ran her finger down the sheet of paper on a clipboard as the seagulls laughed loudly around them and the smell of murky bay water permeated the air. "Margaret, you said?"

Margaret nodded. "Yes, I called and made a reservation for nine at 7 p.m."

The host shook her head as she ran her finger down the

sheet of paper again. "Did you maybe put it under a different name?"

Margaret felt her stomach start to drop. "No. It was definitely under my name."

The host called over Jeremy, her manager, who was busy chatting it up with a table sitting outside.

"How can I help, Ashley?" Jeremy said as he approached with a wide welcoming smile.

Ashley glanced at Margaret. "They said they had a reservation for nine at seven tonight. It's nowhere on this paper, and we're booked solid," she said, glancing at the line forming.

Jeremy held up his finger. "One moment, Ashley," he said as he walked away, then came promptly back. "I'm sorry. There must have been a mix-up with reservations. This doesn't usually happen. I do have enough seating for you outside at that oyster bar. They shuck oysters right in front of you. Honestly, I think it's the best seat in the house."

Margaret turned to the group, who were all nodding. "Let's do it," Liz said as they all followed Jeremy to the bar and took their seats.

"Well, this worked out nicely," Margaret said happily as she dangled her feet from the barstool she sat on.

Dave leaned over and kissed her on the side of her head. "It all worked out perfectly."

They stared at their menus as Dave pulled out the bottles of wine and cans of beer and set them on the bar.

"What can I get youse?" the rough-looking gentleman with a towel across his shoulder said from behind the bar.

Donna looked around. "Do you have wineglasses?"

"Sure do. How many?"

"Well, I think the ladies are having wine and the men are having beer," Donna said, while looking at everyone for a response.

"OK, five wineglasses coming up. By the way, my name is Gary if you need anything."

"Nice to meet you, Gary," Greg said as he studied the menu.

Sarah breathed deeply and closed her eyes before looking towards the wide bay before them. The oyster bar somewhat resembled one of those open-air tiki bars with a thatch roof. It was pretty large too. Even with the nine of them, there was room for ten more people on the other side.

While Margaret poured the wine in the glasses and passed them down, Dave gave the guys their beer. Suddenly, the tall blond oyster crewmen was in sight. He stopped to take off his waders and hung them on a hook at the back of the restaurant, then proceeded to step behind the oyster bar alongside Gary.

"Oh, am I glad to see you, Nick," Gary said. I think we're about to get busy out here. See that line to get in over there?"

Nick nodded as he washed his hands at the sink and towel dried them off. "I did," he said as he glanced back over at the line then over to everyone on the barstools. His eyes met Lisa's again and lingered there for a little too long.

Another group sat on the other side of the bar, and Gary introduced himself, leaving Nick assigned to them. Lisa felt her heart flutter a million beats as she watched him clear the oyster-shucking area that was now his domain. He was so meticulous in where everything was placed, and the man was downright gorgeous—the kind of gorgeous that's intimidating. He had a shirt on, but Lisa could see the chiseled muscles underneath, and even though he had been out on the bay with the oysters, he had an intoxicating salty pine scent, and this cool way about him.

"The name's Nick," he said as he held his hand out first to Dave and Margaret, and then went down the row until he got to Lisa. Lisa put her hand out to touch his and as soon as she did, she felt electric shocks. Not the scary hurtful kind, but the exciting kind.

"Nice to meet you," Lisa said, immediately pulling her hand back and burying her head in the menu.

Nick smiled as he grabbed a bag of oysters that the barback brought up and poured them over the ice in the bin in front of him.

"I think we're ready to order, Nick …" Margaret said as she looked over at everyone, waiting for an affirmative response.

"Yeah, I know what I want," Dale said as he set his menu back on the bar.

"Are you ready, Lisa?" Margaret asked, noticing she still had her head buried deep in the menu.

Lisa put her menu down and nodded at Margaret. "I think so."

Nick bit his lip. "OK … *Lisa*, let's start with you."

Lisa felt her heart skip. He had been paying attention when Margaret said her name. "I'll have a half dozen of the salty fisherman oysters and the wedge salad."

Nick leaned on the counter and propped his head with his hands in front of her, his forearm muscles looking very pronounced. "Great choice. Both favorites of mine."

Lisa tried to breathe, but her chest tightened. "Great," she said in a high-pitched voice that even she had never heard before.

By the time everyone else had ordered, and Nick had gone inside to get their bread and bread plates, Donna nudged Lisa. "You OK over there?"

Lisa shook her head and laughed. "Our bartender looks like a Calvin Klein model."

"Gary?!" Donna asked.

"No, Donna," Lisa said, trying to hold in her laughter.

"Nick?!" Donna yelled out, unknowingly.

Lisa immediately ducked. "Shh! Lower your voice. He's going to hear you."

Donna started laughing as she looked up to meet Nick's eyes as he stood over the oysters chilling on ice.

"Did you need something?" Nick said as he set down the hot baskets of breads with butter plates.

Donna shook her head and giggled. "We're good. Just looking forward to those oysters, Nick."

They watched in awe and wonder as Nick started shucking the oysters. He held an oyster with a towel on a cutting board and did a couple quick maneuvers with the knife and popped it open, then detached the oyster from the bottom of the shell. He did six oysters within minutes and had them plated beautifully on a personal tray of ice with fresh lemon slices and mignonette sauce.

Ten minutes later, they were all eating. "Is everyone enjoying their oysters?" Nick asked as they all dug into their shared trays, except for Lisa who had her own.

Greg wiped his mouth with his napkin. "These are so fresh, and I mean *fresh*. Really the best oysters I've had in a long while."

Dale nodded in agreement. "We both have restaurants here in Cape May and would love to be able to offer these to our guests."

Nick smiled. "That's great. I'm sure we can make that happen."

Sarah pushed the empty tray away from her. "Were you just out on the bay harvesting these?"

Nick nodded. "Not these specific ones, but we were sorting some new oysters that will be served shortly. It really is farm to table here. Oyster farm, that is."

"You do it all, Nick," Margaret said, feeling impressed with his talent.

"You sure do," Dave agreed.

Nick blushed. "Well, thanks. I try. I think your entrees are probably ready. I'm going to head in and get them for you after I clear your oyster trays," he said as he glanced over at Lisa and smiled.

Lisa felt anxiety creeping in and quickly looked at Donna. "So, how many nights are you all staying at the Victorian?"

Donna watched Nick clear their trays and walk away, then she started laughing. "Lisa, I know you know that it's till Monday night."

Lisa rolled her eyes. "I know. I know. It's just … I don't know how to act around him," she said, trying to whisper.

"Why? He's being nice, plus I think he has a *thing* for you," Donna said with a smirk.

Lisa's eyes widened. "You think?"

Donna nodded. "His hand lingered on yours when you shook hands. He took note of your name and remembered it on the first try—even I can barely do that—and I caught him looking at you quite a bit while you were oblivious."

Lisa shook her head. "I think it's all in your head, and if it's not, he's probably like that with every single girl at the bar. Schmoozes and flirts and gets all the tips he wants. I'm sure it's his schtick, and I'm not falling for it."

"OK, everyone, I got a little help bringing your dishes out," Nick said as he held a tray up with one hand and another server followed behind him with a few platters.

After handing out all their dishes, he set Lisa's wedge salad in front of her. "Oh, almost forgot. I requested extra blue cheese on the side for you. It's made in-house, and it's the best. Trust me. I always want a little extra whenever I order this," Nick said, smiling.

Donna chuckled while putting her arm around Lisa's shoulders. "Isn't that so *nice* that he did that, Lisa? So nice."

Lisa gave Donna the side-eye, feeling quite embarrassed of the spectacle she was making. "Yes, thank you, Nick," Lisa said, glancing up at him quickly before stabbing her fork into the wedge of iceberg lettuce drenched in blue cheese, bacon crumbles, and fresh red tomatoes.

Margaret squealed with delight as she looked up from her meal towards the bay that sat before them behind the bar. "Oh my gosh, the sun is starting to set. How amazing is this timing?" Margaret turned her stool so her back was to Dave to get a better look, and Dave wrapped his arms around her, letting her lean back into him as they took a break from eating to watch the colors of the sky change.

Sarah and Chris, Liz and Greg, and Donna and Dale all took that as their cue to do the same, while Lisa continued to eat her wedge salad.

Nick had been in the restaurant for a moment and had just come back with a towel draped over his shoulder. He found a wood beam and leaned his back against it as he took a moment to savor the sunset with everyone else. He sighed deeply, ran his hand through his thick hair, then crossed his arms as though in thought.

Lisa slowly looked up from her salad towards Nick, and he must have seen her as he turned his head. Without a word, he gave Lisa a half-smile, then turned back towards the sunset with his thoughts.

CHAPTER FIVE

By Saturday evening, Judy and Bob were the last to arrive at the Outer Banks beach house after deciding to stop in Cape Charles on the way over for some lunch and shopping.

Bob pulled the car up to the house and noticed the driveway was packed full of vehicles. "Well, where am I going to park?"

Judy glanced to the right. "There are some parking spots in front of this recreational center here. The sign says we can't park overnight, though."

Bob sighed and parked in an empty spot, popped the trunk, and started pulling the luggage out. "Did we really need to bring three coolers of food?"

Judy shrugged. "I wanted to be prepared."

"Fine. Fine. Let's start lugging all this inside," Bob said as he shut the trunk.

Pulling two rolling suitcases behind him, he also carried Judy's beach bag while holding two pillows steady under his armpit. Judy had her purse and one suitcase, as she was afraid to get her newly painted nails scratched up.

Judy's sister Linda stepped out onto the deck and widened

her eyes when she saw Judy and Bob approaching. "Guys, they're finally here," she yelled to everyone inside.

The rest of the bunch stepped outside to look as sweat poured down Bob's face. Judy ran up the stairs to greet everyone, leaving the suitcase at the bottom.

Mike shook his head and walked down the front steps. "Bob, let me help you. We've got an elevator right inside there. No need to climb all these steps."

"Well, thank goodness," Bob said as Mike took two of the suitcases from him.

Phil met them at the elevator. "You don't need to take the elevator in order to drop off the luggage, though, as your room is down here. The coolers, I can take up for you."

Judy arrived from the inside stairwell, overhearing the conversation. "I'm sorry. Our room is *where?*"

Phil pointed down the dark, eerily quiet ground floor hallway, past the pool table. "That door there. Last room on the left. First come, first serve. You know how it goes. Here, I'll take the cooler up to the kitchen for you," Phil said as he stepped inside the elevator and the door shut.

Bob glanced at Judy, disappointment all over her face. "Well, let's go see our room," he said, trying to make her feel better.

Judy sighed as she walked behind Bob to the room. Once inside, they flipped the light on to reveal two twin beds on either side of the room with a tiny window above them that barely let in any light. Up above, in the right-hand corner, was what looked like a small computer screen mounted to the wall.

Bob set the suitcases down, and gesturing to a door inside the room, said, "That must be our bathroom."

Judy opened the door to find a minuscule bathroom decorated for children with stick-on cartoon sea creatures all over the walls and a shower curtain with the same design. "Well, guess we shouldn't have stopped in Cape Charles," she said, feeling utterly annoyed.

Bob wasn't happy about it either, but he knew how much Judy had been looking forward to the time in this house with her family, so he tried to keep the mood positive. "We can always push these beds together. It's not a big deal."

Judy sighed. "I guess you're right," she said as she sat on a bed that had the comfort of a wooden board.

Bob laid on the other twin bed, kicked off his shoes, and snatched the remote off the end table. Pointing it at the tiny screen on the wall, the TV turned on to an old episode of *MASH*."

Judy squinted her eyes. "We're supposed to watch TV on that?"

Bob laughed. "I guess so. Looks like we're watching ants walk around on that TV."

Judy rolled her eyes while getting up, then unzipped her suitcase. "They really give kids' rooms the short end of the stick at these rentals, don't they?"

Bob nodded, finally no longer willing to try and spin a positive outlook on the ridiculous situation. "It stinks."

"Right?!" Judy blurted out, finally happy that Bob was seeing what she was. "I mean, we're in our seventies. Our old bones shouldn't be lying on these tiny board beds. We should have a balcony and an adult bathroom."

Bob stood up. "Do you want me to say something? Who do I talk to about this?"

Judy widened her eyes. "No. *Don't* you say a thing. I don't want to cause any issues. This is Marty and Jane's week, really, not ours."

"Well, alright then. I'm going to get what's left out of the car," Bob said as he left the room.

Judy walked into the bathroom and closed the door behind her. Moments later, another door swung open on the other side of the bathroom.

"Ah! Someone's in here!" Judy belted out.

"Oh, I'm so sorry. I didn't know," a voice said as they slammed the door shut.

Judy's racing heart started to slow down as she realized the door she'd thought was a closet was actually a second door to the bathroom from the hallway. So, technically it wasn't a private bathroom."

"That's OK," Judy said as she quickly stood up and washed her hands.

"Is that my sister Judy?" the voice said from behind the now closed door.

Judy opened the door. "Carol!" she yelled as she gave her a big hug. "I didn't see you initially when we arrived."

"Oh, we just arrived not long ago, and I was unpacking," Carol said motioning to a door across the hallway.

Judy leaned on the door frame. "You're down here with us?"

Carol rolled her eyes. "Yup. Great, isn't it?" she said sarcastically.

Judy felt like a weight had been lifted off her chest. She finally had someone other than Bob to understand her woes. "It's kind of terrible. I would have rather been in our own hotel room, had I known this was going to be our room."

Carol nodded. "I agree. You should see our room."

Judy grabbed Carol's arm. "No, you have to see ours first."

"Oh, I've seen it. It's why I chose our room out of the two, but … let's just say I regret that decision now," Carol said while trying to force a chuckle.

"Oh, really?" Judy said as she followed Carol across the dark hallway to their door.

Carol swung the door open, revealing a pretty boring white-walled room with brown carpet and a queen bed.

"OK, I don't see how this is worse," Judy said, as she stepped inside and looked the room up and down.

Carol shook her head. "Oh, this here is all fine. Our bathroom is the problem," she said as she opened her bathroom door to reveal a toilet with the tank cover off and propped up beside it. "The toilet doesn't work, and neither does the sink. It's why I was trying to use your bathroom."

"You're kidding," Judy said as she glanced around at everything. "Well, did someone call the realtor?"

Carol rolled her eyes. "Oh, we called alright. They can't get anyone out here until Tuesday. We leave on Tuesday. So, it looks like we're sharing a bathroom. I hope you don't mind."

Judy waved her hand in the air. "Oh, it's totally fine. We shared a bathroom growing up as kids all those years, right? It's nothing."

Carol breathed a sigh of relief and put her arm around her sister. "We're only down here to sleep and shower. We'll be fine."

Judy nodded. "You're right. Let's enjoy our time here."

Bob appeared with the last of the luggage. "Everything OK?"

"Oh, everything is fine, Bob. Carol and Jack are across the hall from us. I guess we aren't the only ones down in the dungeon," Judy said while chuckling. Carol burst into a laugh with her until they were both laughing so hard they could barely breathe.

* * *

After dinner at the Oyster Bar, Margaret had the idea to head back to the Victorian and hang out on the front porch to talk and people watch. They had the big, beautiful house for the weekend, they might as well spend *some* time there.

They each found a chair on the porch and got comfortable. Margaret and Dave chose the chair swing while everyone else paired up in love seats or single chairs.

"What I'd give to own a place like this," Chris said as he studied the gingerbread trim along the porch.

Dale nodded in agreement. "If this were my home, I'd sit

out here every night to relax and every morning to eat breakfast."

Everyone let out a sigh, feeling at peace on what felt like the perfect evening to be outside—warm enough not to need a jacket, but cool enough to keep the bugs away.

Margaret and Dave swayed on the chair swing, with Dave's arm around Margaret, when something caught her eye. She watched as a couple walked down the street, dancing and twirling till they got to the front of their house. Then the woman did two high kicks before landing back in the man's arms. She stood up and hugged him, while they both laughed.

Everyone on the porch had been watching along with Margaret, and they all clapped. "Bravo!"

The couple turned to them, looking thoroughly embarrassed, having not realized anyone was watching. "Oh, thank you," the woman said, her face growing red. "We were just practicing."

"Well, you looked great," Margaret said with a wide grin.

"You really did," Liz chimed in.

The guy spoke up. "Well, if you're interested, they're doing dance classes this weekend over at the Blackberry Hotel."

"In the courtyard," the woman said.

"Oh, really?" Margaret asked, curious about it all. "Is there time to sign up, do you think?"

The guy looked at the woman and shrugged, then turned to Margaret. "I don't see why not. They may still be there if you want to walk down and ask. Monday evening is the dance competition."

Margaret glanced at the rest of the group. "Anyone interested?"

Donna raised her hand. "I am, but I'm not a good dancer."

"Oh, we aren't either. It's just something fun to do. I think you all should sign up," the woman said as she grabbed the man's hand.

"Well, thank you for letting us know. We won't keep you

any longer. Enjoy your night," Margaret said as excitement built within her.

"How about it, gentleman? Interested?" Liz asked.

Greg shrugged as he glanced at the guys. "I do too much dancing in the kitchen while stepping around produce boxes, stacks of glasses, and all of that. I think I need a break this weekend," he said with a chuckle.

Chris shook his head. "My knee is still messed up from tripping over the fishing pole on the dock. I think I'm out."

Dale nodded. "I have two left feet. I don't think it will be all that much fun," he said looking over at Dave.

Dave shrugged. "I should probably stay back and hang with the guys so they're not alone. Why don't you all go and report back? We'll come watch you and cheer you on at the competition."

Margaret rolled her eyes, feeling disappointed. It was obvious Sarah, Donna, and Liz weren't that pleased either, but they all understood. It wasn't the guys' thing.

Liz stood up. "How about we head to the hotel and see if we can sign up. I'm sure it won't take long. We'll be right back," she said as she led the way down the steps, followed by the rest of the gals.

It was dark out as they walked down the street towards Beach Avenue. The streets were mostly lit by the soft glow of lampposts in front of the large Victorians that lined the streets. Even though it was May, some houses still had electric candlesticks in every window—there was even one in the tiny window of the attic.

Lisa pointed as they walked towards a dark Victorian lit only by a soft orange glow coming from the front window. "Wow. Stunning, isn't it? The way it's eerie yet whimsical at the same time."

Sarah widened her eyes as she stopped to look. "You're right. These houses have so much history. It's absolutely fascinating.

Margaret pointed ahead to some soft lights in the distance. "There's the hotel. Let's get over there quickly, so we can put our names in before everyone leaves for the evening," she said as she started walking faster.

Minutes later, they found a lady with a tight bun sitting on a chair while pulling off her dancing heels and replacing them with sandals.

"Hi. We're just curious if this is where we sign up for dancing lessons?" Donna asked, looking around. There weren't many people left.

The lady stood up. "It is, but we're full, unfortunately."

"Well, that stinks," Liz said. "Thanks anyway. Figured we'd try."

The lady sighed, noticing they all looked truly disappointed. "How about this. I'll squeeze you in. Be here with bells on tomorrow at 1 p.m."

"For real?" Margaret asked, excitement building inside of her.

"Yes, though, I just realized, I don't have enough instructors. I may have to call my brothers in to help. You'll be paired with a professional dancer that will teach you how to dance. I'll also be instructing the whole group from the front as well. We take this very ... seriously," the lady said as she pulled the pins out of her bun, revealing long waist-length silky brown hair.

"I can't thank you enough. I'm Margaret, that's Donna, then Lisa, Liz, and Sarah. We promise to be here with bells on."

"Now, will your husbands or boyfriends be joining you? We have a lot of couples signed up, which is pretty common," the lady asked.

Liz shook her head. "They aren't interested."

The lady laughed. "That's fine. We have a few women in the same scenario signed up. I'm Natalia. Come dressed to dance, and be ready to sweat," she said while snapping her fingers in the air and twirling. "One o'clock here in the courtyard, and then again Monday morning at eight. Competition is Monday evening at 6 p.m. See you there," she said with a smile as she sashayed towards the hotel.

"Did that just happen?" Liz asked as she stared at the group.

Lisa laughed. "It totally did, and now we'd better show up or this woman might come for us."

Donna rolled her eyes. "Did she say they take this competition *seriously* with only *two* lessons beforehand?'

Sarah nodded and laughed. "That, she *certainly* did."

Margaret led the way out of the courtyard and back to the lamppost-lit street where they took turns twirling each other as they walked and laughed—just like the couple who'd inspired them had done.

"I think we've got this. One of us has got to win this competition," Margaret said.

Donna shrugged. "Even if we don't, who cares? I'm only it for the fun we're about to have."

CHAPTER SIX

Judy and Bob woke up at 5 a.m. Sunday morning due to loud noises coming from above their twin beds, which they decided to not push together since they were leaving Tuesday morning anyway.

"What's that?" Bob asked out loud.

Judy opened one eye and yawned. "Sounds like they're playing musical chairs up there."

The noises only got louder.

"These walls and ceilings are paper thin. *What* is above our bedroom?" Bob asked, flabbergasted.

"I thought it was another bedroom ..." Judy said, not entirely sure.

Bob tried to close his eyes and sleep, but the noises kept coming. "Are they rearranging the bedroom furniture before sunrise? I don't understand what is happening here."

Judy shrugged and rolled over, trying to get a little more shut-eye.

Suddenly, the noises stopped, and it was quiet again. They both started to drift off, when *bam!* It sounded like a bowling ball had been dropped.

"That's it. I'm getting up," Bob said as he sat up from the

bed, swinging his legs over the edge. "Ow," he said, holding his back.

Judy took her glasses from the nightstand and put them on. "Are you OK?"

Bob chuckled but that caused the pain to be even worse. "I think I slept weird."

Judy sat up and pushed her feet into her slippers that were right next to the bed. "No, you slept fine. It's the children's bed that's the issue. They are made with mattresses carved out of wood, I'm telling ya."

Bob laughed again. "Ow. Stop making me laugh," he said as he tried to stand up.

Judy pointed to the bathroom. "Go get a hot shower. I'm sure that'll fix you right up."

Bob yawned as he headed to the bathroom, then opened the shower curtain to turn the water on. "What in the—?"

Judy hopped out of bed. "OK, now what?"

"There's mold all over this shower. What cleaners did they hire?" Bob asked, frustration growing by the minute.

Judy pushed her way through to see, swinging the curtain open wider. "Oh. Ewwww … you know what, go to the cleaning supply closet upstairs and grab some cleaner and a scrub brush. I'll have this sparkling in ten minutes."

Bob nodded. "Sure thing, dear."

An hour later, the bathroom was probably the cleanest it'd been in months, and they were showered, dressed, and upstairs with a handful of the family members, who were busy getting breakfast prepared.

"What can we do to help?" Judy asked.

Debbie wiped her hands with a kitchen towel. "Well, Marty and Jane went out to Duck Donuts for those piping-hot dough-nuts we love. We've got an egg casserole in the oven, Phil is cooking the bacon and sausage, Linda is making the French toast, and I guess that leaves the fruit. Would you cut it up and make a fruit salad?"

"Sure. We can do that," Bob said as he maneuvered around everyone to the small island in the middle of the kitchen with a cutting board.

Judy opened the fridge, found the fruit, pulled it out, and brought it to the sink to be washed.

Bob opened a drawer while looking for a knife and inadvertently ripped the entire drawer out, dropping it and the silverware it held all over the floor and on people's feet. "Oh, I'm so sorry about that," he said, bending over to pick it up.

Judy brought a colander full of strawberries over to Bob, but he turned at the same time, causing the colander to fly out of Judy's hands and into Linda, who was luckily wearing an apron.

Bob rolled his eyes. "You know what? How about I sit this one out. I'm going over there." He pointed to the living room where Jane and Marty's parents, along with Jack, were starting a 1500-piece jigsaw puzzle on a large coffee table.

"OK, dear," Judy said with a slight chuckle to ease the tension.

Bob took a seat on the couch next to the puzzle. "Need some help?"

"Yes, we do," Charles, Marty's dad, said with a laugh, as he held up the front of the box. "See this here. It's a picture turned into a puzzle."

Bob studied it. "Looks like a photo of Marty and Jane."

"Yep," Bertha, Jane's Mom, said. "Do you see the issue with it, though?"

Bob looked again at the photo. "They're both wearing all blue and standing next to blue siding."

"Bingo!" Jack said as she searched for the edge and corner pieces. "Everything is the same color in the puzzle except their white shoes and skin. This is going to be the most difficult puzzle I've ever done—and I do a lot of them."

Charles bit his lip while he stared over the puzzle pieces as though he were trying to will them together. "Well, thank you to whoever brought this one," he yelled sarcastically towards the kitchen.

"Marty and Jane brought it, and they're out getting doughnuts. You can thank them when they get back," Linda yelled.

Charles rolled his eyes. "Alright, folks. Let's get this puzzle done pronto so we can start the next one, which will be much more fun."

"Oh, what is it?" Bob asked.

Bertha smiled. "It's a beautiful beach scene much like the one out here where Marty and Jane are to be married tomorrow."

Bob glanced outside, noticing the live oak trees dancing wildly in the wind. "That's great. Looking forward to the nuptials."

Charles's wife, Tracy, was quiet the whole time as she concentrated on doing the puzzle. Meanwhile, Bertha's husband, Hank, had taken a break to the read the Sunday paper out on the deck.

After fifteen minutes of working, Bob broke the silence. "So, besides the nuptials tomorrow, what are the rest of the plans this weekend? I need to be filled in."

Bertha cleared her throat. "Well, after breakfast, we have reservations for a jeep ride on the beach to see the horses. I believe Judy said you two were going. Then, tonight, we're all contributing to dinner, a potluck of sorts. Early tomorrow morning, a handful of us are going to pick up the arbor they'll be married under and decorate it with flowers while more friends and family arrive. They have rooms booked at a nearby hotel. The nuptials will be at 11 a.m. out on the beach, then afterwards, we're having food catered here for everyone. A band is coming and setting up by the pool. It's going to be great."

Just then, Marty and Jane walked in with two huge boxes of hot doughnuts. "The main course is here, everyone," Marty said jokingly as he set them on the long dining room table.

"Perfect timing—we're ready to eat," Debbie said as she finished placing the last table setting.

More people came in from outside and up from downstairs, and within moments, everyone was sitting at the table enjoying breakfast.

Jane tapped her glass with a fork to get everyone's attention. "We just wanted to thank you all for being here for our wedding. It just so happened Marty's friend who owns this house had the week free and generously offered to let us use it for the celebration."

Marty smiled at Jane. "We're really excited about finally being able to call each other husband and wife ...."

Just then, a large black poodle bounded up the steps towards the dining room table.

"Squishy! So glad you joined us," Jane said. "This is our dog. You may have heard her romping around the room early this morning. If so, I apologize. She has her ritual zoomies every morning at 5 a.m. on the dot."

Bob glanced at Judy with a smirk. There it was. It was dog releasing energy by running at full speed, not musical chairs after all.

* * *

Meanwhile in Cape May, Dale cooked breakfast for the group while everyone sat on the front porch with their coffees.

Donna closed her eyes and inhaled. "I smell bacon."

Sarah nodded. "I do too. I guess bacon is on the menu."

"Is he really not telling us what he's making?" Chris asked.

Margaret nodded as she took a sip of her hot coffee. "He wants it to be a surprise."

Greg shook his head. "He needs some help. I'm going in ...."

Liz tried to reach for Greg's hand to pull him back, but it was too late. The screen door to the inside had slammed closed as Greg made his way to the temporarily forbidden kitchen.

They all waited in silence to hear what would happen next. Nothing did for a minute … and then '80s music started playing from the inside speakers.

Liz laughed. "Looks like Greg got in. That's his music playing from the kitchen."

Twenty minutes later, Dale was at the screen door, untying his apron. "Come and get it … if you're hungry that is," he said with a smile.

They all jumped up from the porch, ready to devour whatever he had cooked up, and made their way to the dining room. There was avocado toast, scrambled eggs, bacon, and piping-hot cinnamon rolls.

"Dale, this looks amazing," Lisa said as she pulled up a seat to the table alongside everyone else.

After finishing and helping clean up, everyone got changed and ready for their Cape May beach day. Luckily, they were only a block from the ocean, making it a nice easy walk to Broadway Beach.

They found their spot on the sand, set up their chairs, umbrellas, and blankets and then got comfortable. Greg turned on some music with his portable speaker, and Chris manned the cooler, handing out whatever anyone needed at a moment's notice, while Dave was in charge of keeping the umbrella steady when the wind picked up, because the ladies were busy chatting it up.

"So, Dale and Donna … are you excited for the wedding?" Liz asked as she took a sip of lime seltzer.

Donna smiled as she looked over at Dale, who had completely laid back his chair and was already staring at the inside of his eyelids. "Are we excited for the wedding, Dale?"

Dale sat straight up. "Of course we are. A July 4 wedding. It's going to come with its own firework show, free of charge. Can't beat it."

Donna laughed. "Dale is sick of talking about the wedding. We've been planning nonstop for weeks. It has literally taken over our life. I guess that's what happens when you make the decision to not wait too long for the big day. Aside from a couple vendors we're waiting to hear from, we seem to be all set. I'm excited."

Margaret sighed happily. "It's going to be magical. I can feel it. We can't wait for your big day."

Liz turned to Sarah. "I know you and Chris are taking the wedding plans much slower, right?"

Sarah glanced at Chris. "Yeah, we want to have lots of time to plan and make it perfect. I'm fine with that, plus we're really focused on the Book Nook and the Blue Heron Birding Boat lately."

Chris nodded. "I'm thinking about finally adding a second boat and captain, and Sarah has started hosting different types of classes over at the bookshop."

"Next week we're having a pottery class, if anyone wants to join," Sarah chimed in.

Lisa squealed. "You're kidding! I've been looking for a pottery class. I'm in."

Dave took notice of Lisa's surfboard that she had taken off the roof of her van and brought with her. "You surfing today, Lisa?"

Lisa looked out towards the waves. "I'm thinking about it. I may have to throw on my wetsuit, though. Not sure of the water temperature."

"I hear it's pretty warm already," Liz said as she looked at the dark-blue water.

"Well, I'd better give it a go, then. I haven't surfed in months. These waves don't even compare to what we were surfing in Hawaii every day," Lisa said as she got up and grabbed her surfboard. "I'll be back."

Lisa made her way down the beach towards the water. A group of surfers were out there already, and her long blonde hair blew in the wind as she stopped to watch. Someone caught her eye, and that someone seemed to be looking right back at her. Lisa shielded the sun from her eyes with her hand. In Hawaii, all the surfers knew each other. Here, she wasn't sure if she was imposing or not—it was a community of its own for sure.

If she paddled out there, would she be an outcast? She stood her surfboard in the sand and watched a little more to figure out her plan. When a surfer sitting on his board waved to her, she looked closer and realized it was Nick, the gorgeous blond oyster farmer. Her heart started beating fast as she waved back. He signaled for her to come out to him with his hands. Lisa took that as her sign and paddled her way out past the breaking waves until she was next to Nick.

"Hey. Lisa, right?" Nick asked as he sat on his board, legs hanging in the water on either side of it, bobbing over the small waves.

Lisa smiled. "You've got a good memory, Nick."

Nick was taken aback. She had remembered his name as well. "Well, I can say the same about you."

"How are the waves today?" Lisa asked, noticing how the water made Nick's muscles glisten in the sunlight.

Nick laughed. "Not that good. I've been sitting here a while, waiting for the perfect one. I caught a few duds, though Johnny over there got a good one," he said pointing to some surfers next to them.

Lisa laughed. "So, why'd you call me out here then?"

Nick shrugged. "I wanted to talk to you, I guess."

Lisa felt her face grow red. She turned to look the other way, not knowing what to say to that.

"Are you from around here? I've never seen you before," Nick asked.

"Actually, I grew up here, but moved away for college and ended up in Hawaii. Surfed just about every day for years and years," Lisa said as she ran her fingers through her wet hair.

"You're kidding. Hawaii? I can already tell you're probably a better surfer than me. That's really neat," Nick said, thoroughly impressed. "What brought you back here?"

Lisa bit her nail. Here it was. *The* question. "I got divorced and needed to get out of Hawaii. Where I lived was very tight-knit, everyone knew each other, and I knew if he stayed, I'd have to leave. So, I took my old VW Bus on a trip of a lifetime across the country with my destination being Cape May, my first home. I have no idea what I'm going to do after Cape May, though. I'm just letting myself figure it out as it happens."

Nick's eyes widened. "Just when I thought you couldn't possibly be any cooler."

Lisa laughed. "Enough about me. What about you? Are you from here?"

Nick nodded. "I am, originally, but we moved around a bit. Spent about ten years in Maine working on lobster boats, then found my passion was oysters and ended up back in Cape May. I actually run the oyster farm over by Joe's Oyster Bar."

"You do? Well, talk about interesting. I enjoyed watching you all work out there the other night," Lisa said.

Nick smiled. "We have another oyster farm over near Highs Beach in Cape May Court House. Would you be interested in seeing it sometime?"

"Definitely," Lisa said.

Nick looked out towards the beach in thought. "Is ... tomorrow good?"

Lisa paused for a moment. "Well, I'm spending time with a group of friends this weekend. Then, we have this dance competition thing tomorrow evening."

Nick laughed. "Dance competition? Never heard of one of those around here. Sounds fun. Well, how about this. Tell your friends to come too. I'm sure they'll enjoy it. It's a really incredible spot right on the bay. We have to go at low tide, though. That should be around twelve."

Just then, Lisa turned to see a large wave coming right at

them. She paddled hard to catch it, as did Nick. By the time the wave broke, Lisa was surfing like a professional and Nick had missed the wave completely. She ended her ride near the shoreline, thirty feet away from him. "It's a plan, Nick," Lisa yelled out as she stood up in the water and headed back towards the beach.

"Wait. I need your number," Nick yelled back from the ocean.

Lisa loudly said her number, but figured it was useless. How was Nick going to remember it, he had nothing to write on, and his cell phone certainly wasn't with him.

"Maybe we can meet here?" Lisa said while gesturing at Nick.

"I'll pick you up," Nick said with a wide smile.

Lisa smiled back and headed to the group, having not felt that kind of thrill in years. Not even when she surfed the huge fifty-foot wave in Maui.

CHAPTER SEVEN

"You're telling me that Nick, the cute guy from the oyster bar, was in the ocean with you surfing?" Donna asked Lisa, bewildered, as the ladies walked to their dance lesson.

"And you didn't say a word about it until now?" Sarah asked, highly confused.

Lisa shrugged and chuckled. "You all were in a deep conversation when I came back, I didn't want to interrupt."

Liz laughed. "You should have interrupted. Greg would have talked all day about Heirloom, and I hear about his restaurant all the time."

"And Dale too. Don't forget he jumped in there to talk about his restaurant too," Donna said, chuckling.

Sarah interrupted. "I must have been too engrossed with my book. I missed it. How are their restaurants doing?"

"Just fine!" Donna and Liz yelled out in unison, then promptly looked at each other, while cracking up.

"No, seriously, though. Dale had some kinks to work out this past spring, but he has great managers now that are running the restaurant like a well-oiled machine," Donna said.

"And Greg's restaurant is doing better than ever," Liz announced.

"So happy about the restaurants, now let's get back to Nick. I've been waiting for Lisa to finish filling in the details," Margaret interrupted.

Lisa felt starry-eyed as she recounted the run-in with Nick. "Well, we talked some, and then he asked if I'd like to see his other oyster farm over near Highs Beach in Cape May Court House. He invited everyone. Are you guys interested? It would be tomorrow around low tide at noon."

"Definitely," Sarah said, as the rest of the ladies nodded affirmatively.

Donna nudged Lisa as they stepped through the hotel gates towards the courtyard. "He likes you."

Liz laughed. "Saying he likes her sounds so fourth grade. Is that how we say it now as adults?"

Donna shrugged. "OK, how about this … I think Nick is interested in getting to know you, Lisa."

Lisa smiled. "We'll see. He may be like this with all the girls."

As they approached the lush green grass in the secluded courtyard, which was bordered by tall evergreens and trees, they saw Natalia wave at them from the huge dance floor that was placed over a cement patio.

"Over here, ladies," Natalia said as she watched the professional dance instructors pair off with their students.

"What did we get ourselves into?" Margaret asked as she watched the professional dancers stretching their legs and arms as though they were getting ready for an all night dance-a-thon.

Natalia paired all of them with a male dance partner except Margaret. She was the lone one left.

"I'm short an instructor," Natalia said, feeling frustrated as she searched the courtyard. "Where is my brother? Vinny said he'd be here."

One of Natalia's other brothers, who was paired with Lisa,

shrugged. "You know Vin, always working on his own schedule."

Natalia shook her head. "Well, that's not going to fly. Guess I'll be your partner for now, Margaret," she said just as a noise interrupted her.

"Hello everyone!" a voice yelled from across the courtyard.

The group collectively turned to see a dark-haired man with shoulder-length greased-back hair dressed in black slacks, a black button-down shirt, and dance shoes holding a coffee.

"Well, look what the cat dragged in," Natalia said, shaking her head.

Vinny approached, smelling heavily of cologne and displaying a smile. "My dear Natalia. I apologize. You know I need my coffee before anything dance-related."

Natalia rolled her eyes, then pointed to Margaret. "Vinny, you're with Margaret for the weekend."

Vinny's eyes looked Margaret up and down. "Well, I'm not going to complain about that. Nice to meet you, beautiful Margaret," he said while holding his other hand out for a handshake.

"And you as well … Vinny," Margaret said, noticing she had the most boisterous partner out of everyone.

Vinny put his coffee down and rolled up his sleeves while doing a few warm-up stretches. "Have you danced before, Margaret?"

Margaret shrugged. "Not like this."

"Well, we're going to change that this weekend. Get ready to move those hips," he said while twisting his body and snapping his fingers.

Donna, Sarah, Liz, and Lisa all looked at each other and laughed. Margaret was surely in for a wilder ride than they were.

Natalia got out her megaphone. "OK, everyone. We've got about twenty couples out here, so instead of losing my voice, I'm using this megaphone. We have an hour-long lesson today.

Make sure to learn as much as you can from your professional dance partner," she said as she turned on the music. "For those that are new, we're doing the ballroom waltz."

A slow pop song played over the speakers as the instructors started teaching their partners the box step.

Vinny put his arm around Margret's back and took her other hand in his, initiating the steps. "Follow my lead. Step right foot back, slide to the side with the left …. You are going to rise and fall as you step."

Margaret didn't have a clue what she was doing but following Vinny's lead seemed to work. She was dancing the waltz, and as she glanced around the dance floor, it appeared her friends were too.

"Great job, Margaret," Vinny said as he smiled while they danced. "Remember elbows and your head position."

Margaret quickly corrected her posture and laughed. She couldn't believe they were actually doing this.

"Fall into my arms after I twirl you," Vinny said as he took her hand and twirled her a couple times.

Margaret fell back into his arms and Vinny leaned over her, staring into her eyes before pulling her back up to standing position where they went back into the box step.

"Did you like that move?" Vinny asked, feeling proud of himself and pulling her a little closer.

Margaret suddenly felt like this dance lesson was getting a little too close for comfort, but maybe that was just how dancing was.

Natalia walked around the dance floor, eyeing each dancing couple, and giving her critiques and praises. When she got to Margaret and Vinny, she gave Vinny a stern look. "Ballroom waltz, Vinny. None of this other stuff mixed in that you like to do, and no funny business."

Vinny rolled his eyes as he twirled Margaret again. "Sister, why don't you trust me?"

Natalia rolled her eyes as she stepped to the front of the

dance floor and got out the megaphone. "Great lesson today everyone. I saw improvement from the beginning of the lesson to the end with a lot of you. We are finished for the day. We have some bottles of water if anyone would like to grab one. Remember: tomorrow, 8 a.m. is our second lesson and 6 p.m., the big competition."

Margaret thanked Vinny and started to head over to her friends, but Vinny grabbed her hand at the last second. "See you tomorrow, Margaret," Vinny said, letting his hand linger on hers.

Margaret awkwardly pulled her hand away and turned to meet the ladies who were all staring at her.

"What was that all about?" Liz asked Margaret as they walked back to the Victorian.

"What?" Margaret asked, not sure of what Liz was talking about.

Donna butted in. "I think Liz is asking about that Italian stallion you were paired with. He seems loud and aggressive."

Margaret shrugged. "I guess he was, but he seems harmless .... Maybe just overly flirtatious. How were your dance instructors?"

"Good," they all said together.

"I don't think any of us got called beautiful or had our hand grabbed as we were leaving the lesson, though," Sarah said laughing.

* * *

A skinny older man with an unlit cigarette hanging from his lip leaned against the jeep in Corolla, North Carolina. "Alright, I hear y'all want to see some wild horses," he said as he spit into the tall grass behind him.

"That's right. Can't wait," Linda said, glancing around at everyone else.

"OK, then. Well, each jeep fits fifteen people in the back,

so y'all will be in two separate jeeps. Kyle is driving that one, and I—I'm Leonard—will be driving this one. I call her Pearl. Ain't she a beaut? Hop on in and buckle up. It's going to be a wild ride," Leonard said as he smacked the jeep.

He then stood by the steps at the back of the jeep, helping anyone who needed it while boarding.

Judy squished in between Bob and Linda, their whole side of the family was in the same jeep, while Marty and Jane and their immediate family boarded in the other.

"Where did you find this horse excursion?" Judy asked Linda.

Linda shrugged. "Mike found it. It was a bargain compared to the other places around here."

Bob laughed. "I can see why."

Leonard hopped into the front seat of the jeep and turned around to talk to everyone through his back window. The group sat in an uncovered portion of the jeep outfitted with benches that wrapped around the interior. "OK, we're going to head down this road for a bit until we get to the beach. Then, off we go looking for horses. I'll do my best to find 'em."

Moments later, the jeeps left and flew down the road. Wind whipped their hair everywhere. Bob's hat flew off and landed in Mike's face.

"I think you're missing something," Mike said, handing the hat back.

Bob laughed, then stuffed the hat into Judy's purse.

After ten minutes and what felt like being in a wind tunnel, they arrived at the beach.

"Finally, we're here," Judy said as she tried to fix her wind-blown hair.

"Now we can take it nice and slow and look for horses," Bob said as he dug around in Judy's purse for his hat.

Instead, Leonard gunned it down the beach. "Hold on. We might hit a bump or two," he said, cackling when everyone bobbed up and down.

Carol put her hood up and tied the drawstrings so it wrapped tightly around her head.

Fifteen minutes later, they'd flown down the windy beach and, after hitting bump after bump, *finally* found some horses.

Leonard slowed the jeep down. "Well, there they are. Get out your cameras and snap a few photos."

Everyone snapped away. How neat it was to see wild horses on the beach while out on a jeep.

"OK, we're heading out to find more," Leonard said as he gunned the jeep again.

Judy looked behind them to see Kyle in his jeep merrily driving along with Marty and Jane and their crew. How peaceful they looked compared to the roller-coaster ride of a driver Leonard was.

They drove another ten minutes without seeing any other horses, so Leonard drove up towards the beach houses behind the dunes. Here were the houses that actually sat on the beach —no paved roads, just sand and dirt.

Leonard stopped the jeep to everyone's relief, then turned and pointed at a dilapidated house on tall pillars. "See this one? It was totally taken over by that last hurricane we had." He pointed to the top of the pillars. "The water was to about there during the storm. Half of it blew into the ocean. Gone."

Bob shuddered at the thought of someone riding out the storm in that house. Most likely nobody did, but how scary that would have been.

"Leonard, you there?" a voice said on his radio.

Leonard picked up his radio and pushed a button. "What's good, Kyle?"

"I'm told there's lots of horses back by the Christmas house. I'm headed that way," Kyle said.

"Alright, Kyle. I'm headed behind you," Leonard said as he gunned it over a large sand hill.

Some twists and turns later, they finally arrived at the Christmas house, an aptly named beach house painted bright red with green trim, boasting a Christmas tree in the living room's bay window. In front of the house were around ten wild horses.

"Wow, what a sight to be seen," Judy said as she snapped photos with her cell phone.

The group was in awe of the beautiful creatures living so peacefully on the beach and within the little beach house community.

Leonard got out of the jeep, his unlit cigarette still dangling from his lips. "How about I get a group picture of y'all? Did you want to get out and stand over here?" he asked as he gestured to a spot that would have the horses in the distant view.

"Well that sounds like a great idea," Phil said as he hopped out of the jeep, followed by the rest of their group as well as Marty and Jane's group.

"Here, you can use my phone," Debbie said as she handed it to Leonard.

"Well, jeez, these new phones are confusing ...." Leonard said as he tried to figure out how to work it. "I'm used to my flip phone. All the crazy technology these days is out of hand."

The group stood together, smiling and waiting for Leonard.

"Do you want me to show you?" Debbie asked.

Leonard waved her off. "No, no. I've got it," he said as he aimed the phone. "OK, that's going to be a good one. I know it," Leonard said as he walked towards the jeep's steps and handed the phone back to Debbie. "Let me help you all get seated so we can head back."

They all got into the jeep and Leonard slipped into the driver's seat, driving them around the sandy back roads as though they were on a NASCAR racecourse.

"I'm going to throw up," Linda said as she leaned her head on Judy's shoulder. "Let me know when we get back. I'm going to close my eyes."

Twenty minutes later, after being on one of the craziest

rides they'd ever been on, they were finally back where they started—and couldn't have been happier to be out of the jeep.

When Kyle's jeep quietly turned into the driveway, it was apparent he'd gotten the memo to drive slow and carefully. As they all got into their cars to head back to their beach house in Duck, Debbie looked at her cell phone photos in the back seat of Judy and Bob's car.

"How did the group shot come out?" Judy asked.

"I haven't gotten to that photo yet. Let me see …," Debbie said as she swiped the screen. "Well, I don't see a group photo in here. That's strange."

"Are you sure? Can I see?" Judy asked as she reached her hand back towards Debbie. Debbie handed her the phone.

Judy looked at the photos, then started laughing so hard she could barely talk. "There's like six shots of Leonard looking into the camera. He had the lens pointed the wrong way the whole time."

Debbie started laughing. "Are you kidding me? We should have had Kyle take the photos. What were we thinking?"

Bob chuckled. "Well, I'm thinking we don't go with the bargain place next time."

CHAPTER EIGHT

Margaret draped herself on the living room's chaise next to Donna, Lisa, and Liz and rubbed her sore feet. "I'm not wearing those shoes again for the lesson tomorrow. I already have blisters on my toes."

Sarah laid on the couch doing the same. "You're telling me. I'd rather dance barefoot."

Donna laughed. "Well, we'll grab some bandages while we were out, and we'll be good as new for the dance lesson tomorrow morning."

"I sure hope so," Liz said as she stared up at the ceiling.

Margaret crinkled her brow. "Where are the guys, by the way?"

Liz sat up. "They went walking around. Greg wanted to go see the new restaurant a couple blocks down. They should be back any min—"

The front door opened to a boisterous bunch of men laughing and talking. They all caught a glimpse of the gals on the couches.

"How'd the dance lesson go?" Dave asked as he walked over and put his hand on Margaret's shoulder.

"It was nice … we're just a little sore," Margaret smiled.

The ladies nodded in agreement.

Sarah chimed in. "Yeah, our dance partners are an *interesting* bunch, that's for sure."

"What do you mean?" Chris asked.

Sarah chuckled. "They're all super into dancing. They are anything but plain and boring … and then there's Margaret's dance partner. He's a piece of work."

Dave glanced at Margaret. "A piece of work, eh?" he said while laughing.

Margaret nodded. "Definitely."

Greg interrupted, not being able to hold his news. "I've got some plans for us."

"Oh yeah?" Liz asked.

"While the guys and I were out, I ran into a regular customer of mine over at my restaurant. Turns out, he owns a cherry farm about fifteen minutes from here. We can go cherry picking, then walk around the farm. How about it?" Greg asked.

Liz shifted her eyes. "Sounds great, hon, but what are we going to do with all the cherries afterwards?"

Greg shrugged. "I don't know. We'll figure it out. I'm sure they'll last a few days, so we'll take some home to the kids. It just sounds … fun."

"I'm in. I love cherries," Lisa said as she got up from the couch.

"Let's do it," Margaret said as Dave helped her up from chaise.

* * *

Driving up a secluded dirt road bordered by hundreds of cherry trees, all along the road were handwritten signs that had arrows and **Cherries** written on them.

Chris and Greg pulled the two vehicles up the road until they got to a gentleman who directed them to park at the edge of the cherry trees. Across from where they parked was a tent with a couple employees sitting on stools looking at their phones.

After they all got out, they approached the tent.

The young girl on her phone quickly put it away. "Hi! Looking to cherry pick?"

"Yes, we are," Greg said.

The girl reached down and grabbed a handful of big bags, then gave them to Greg. "Perfect. Here're your bags. The cherries are $3.50 a pound."

The gentleman that helped them park was now next to the girl. "Have you all cherry picked before?"

They all shook their heads.

The gentleman picked up two clusters of cherries. "Well, sweet cherries don't ripen after you pick them. So, what you pick is what you get most of the time. You are looking for these dark-red-colored cherries. They will be the ripest and sweetest, unlike these light-red ones here," he said holding the cherries up for everyone to see. "Also, you want to pick the cherries with the stem on them. It keeps them fresh longer."

"Huh, I never knew that," Chris said as he studied the cherries.

"Now, you guys should head about four rows down to find a good amount of cherries. These other rows have been picked over. Have fun," the man said as he watched them head off.

They broke off into pairs, except Lisa, who joined forces with Dale and Donna.

As the group turned down the fourth row of cherry trees, Dave took Margaret's hand. "I've got an idea. Let's head to the sixth row. That way we're not on top of everyone else."

"Great minds think alike," Margaret said as she eyed up some ladders all around the cherry trees.

They got to the sixth row, and Margaret's eyes widened. "I think we hit the jackpot. Look at all those dark-red cherry clusters. Let's get to picking."

Underneath a tall tree, they found not only some shade from the direct sunlight that was baking the field, but there also dangled hundreds of ripe cherries above their heads.

Dave pulled some cherries off and put them in their bag. "How neat is this? I've only been strawberry picking. Never even thought to go cherry picking."

Margaret nodded, thoroughly enjoying the little event Greg had planned. She pulled off a huge cluster of cherries, then studied them. "We'll have to bring the girls. They would love this."

"They definitely would," Dave said as he searched around for the next cluster to pick.

Margaret stopped and stared at Dave. "Are you sure you don't want to try the dance lessons with me?"

Dave stumbled on his words. "Well ... I don't know ...."

"I get it. Not your thing. I won't force you to do something you don't want to."

Dave's heart sank, but he tried to quickly change the subject. "Tell me about this instructor of yours."

Margaret laughed. "Vinny. Oh, he's ... something."

Dave arched his eyebrow. "How so?"

Margaret shook her head, trying to find the words to describe him. "He's just very ... flirty."

Dave shifted his eyes. He wasn't the jealous type *at all*, but Margaret clearly had a wedding ring on, so that was quite a bold move of Vinny.

"Honestly, I feel like he's that way with everyone. I get that vibe," Margaret said trying to ease the tension.

"I'm sure he probably is," Dave said with a laugh. "Well, regardless, I'm glad you ladies found a fun activity to do together this weekend."

Margaret smiled. "What about you fellas? What's your fun male activity?"

Dave shrugged. "Chris wanted to check out a golf course, maybe play a round. Then, there was some talk of other things. We'll see if any of it comes to fruition. I think most of us are fine with just hanging out, talking, listening to music, and relaxing."

"Totally. I get it," Margaret said as she looked down, noticing she was stepping on a lot of squashed cherries.

Dave glanced at her shirt. "Were you eating cherries, Marg?"

Margaret looked at her shirt, then laughed. "No, I was not. I'm covered in cherry juice. How did that happen?"

Dave looked at his shirt. "So am I!"

They both pointed at each other laughing. Then, Dave pulled her in for a hug and kiss.

"Dave and Margaret, where are you?" a voice called from a couple rows down.

"Over here," Margaret yelled.

The group made their way to Dave and Margaret, showing off their full bags of cherries.

"Well, *that* was fun. We're definitely coming back," Sarah said as she popped a cherry in her mouth.

"These are delicious," Donna said, chewing a bite as well. "I never knew we had such delicious cherries grown right here in New Jersey."

* * *

That evening after dinner, the ladies staying in Duck decided to get in the hot tub with drinks.

Judy got in first, carefully submerging to find a seat right in front of a jet that felt like a full-blown massage on her back. "Oh, whoever had this idea is a genius," she said as she held onto her beverage and put her head back on the edge to rest.

Linda, Debbie, Carol, Jane, Bertha, Tracy, and Jane's cousin Jen, all got into the huge hot tub as well.

Linda laid her head back and stared up at the big night sky

above them. "Look at those stars. I can see the Big Dipper. There it is," she said pointing.

Everyone looked up to see.

"There's Jupiter," Jane said, squinting up at the sky. "It looks like a big bright star."

Just then, the guys came outside with cigars and leaned over the deck. "Hello, ladies," Marty said as Jack lit his cigar.

"Hello, my husband-to-be!" Jane yelled back.

"How's the water? Warm?" Bob asked.

"Very," they all said in unison, then started laughing.

The guys stood on the upper deck talking and smoking their cigars, too far away for the ladies to hear what they were saying.

"Are you excited for tomorrow?" Carol asked Jane.

Jane thought for a moment. "Yeah ..."

Judy glanced at Debbie to see if she noticed the hesitation in Jane's voice. Debbie glanced back, signaling she also heard it.

Jane looked around at everyone. "I'm so excited for the party tomorrow. I have friends coming in. They'll be here all week with us. It's going to be so much fun."

Just then, a loud commotion came from the guys on the upper deck.

"What's going on up there?" Carol asked as she stared up at them.

Judy crinkled her nose. "What's that smell?"

Now they all smelled it, and as they looked around, they noticed some bushes on fire on the other side of the yard.

The guys came bounding down the stairs with someone holding a huge pot of water. Marty took it and heaved it on the bushes, promptly extinguishing the fire.

The ladies stayed in the tub since they were not sure what to do, but the situation seemed handled.

Then Marty walked over to the hot tub with his empty pot and leaned on it, panting. "I think someone's cigar ashes lit the bush on fire. Actually … I think it was mine. I accidentally flicked my butt over there."

Tracy crossed her arms. "Accidentally? I sure hope so. I know no son of mine would be throwing his cigar butts all over this property."

Marty nodded. "The guys and I are going in to watch the baseball game. Enjoy yourselves," he said, patting the side of the hot tub, then he headed back up the stairs.

"I probably should get inside too," Tracy said as Bertha followed her out of the hot tub.

"See you all," Bertha said as she wrapped a towel around herself.

As soon as they were inside, Jane let out a groan. "Thank goodness they left. I have stuff I *need* to talk about with you all."

Judy widened her eyes and took a sip of her wine. "What do you mean?"

"Ugh. Where do I even start?" Jane said as she gulped the rest of her wine and set the glass on the edge.

"Start wherever you want to. Just let it out," Carol said, thinking Jane was having issues with her mother.

Jane thought for a moment, then belted it out. "I don't know if I should marry Marty. In fact, I think it's a bad decision."

"What? Are you serious?" Jane's cousin Jen asked, clearly shocked.

Linda looked at Judy, unsure of what to think, then back at Jane. "What are you talking about? The wedding is tomorrow."

Jane took a deep breath as though trying to compose herself. "I think Marty is still in love with his ex-wife, Talia. There, I said it out loud."

"Talia?" Debbie asked, confused. "I don't see how that's possible. Wasn't he the one that wanted the divorce?"

Jane tried to whisper, but it wasn't working. "I found a

photo of her in his wallet. An old photo. Does he have any photos of me in there? Nope."

"Hmm ... that's odd," Judy said, feeling slightly uncomfortable since they were much closer to Marty, their cousin, than they were to Jane. If they had to pick sides, they would have to go with family first, and that was Marty, technically.

Jane rolled her eyes. "That's not all. When we first started dating, all he did was talk about her. It was 'Talia this' and 'Talia that.' I had to finally ask him to please stop talking about his ex-wife. He clearly *wasn't* over her."

"That's strange," Debbie said as she started looking for the hot tub exit to get out of the awkward situation.

"I'm sure it will all work out. Put all of that behind you," Judy said. She didn't know what was going on, but she knew Marty loved Jane.

Linda stood up. "Agreed. Well, I think it's time for me to get out of the hot tub ...."

"Me too," Carol said, following Linda.

Jane started sobbing. "I knew I shouldn't have brought it up. You all clearly don't want to hear it."

Linda and Carol slowly sat back down in the hot tub. "Look, I think you really need to talk to Marty about this. We're not the ones you need to discuss this with."

Jane sobbed so loud, the entire neighborhood could probably hear.

Marty flew out onto the deck. "What's going on?" he yelled down to Jane. "I heard you crying over the loud baseball game."

Jane waved her hand in the air. "I'm fine. Go back inside."

Judy shook her head. "No, she's not. Get on down here, Marty."

Jane wiped her eyes and stared at Judy. "I can't tell him any of this. I can't."

"You have to," Judy said. "We're going to leave and give you two privacy. If there is any time to discuss this with Marty, it's now—the day *before* your wedding." Judy followed the rest of the ladies out of the hot tub.

Marty hurried down the steps to Jane, now alone in the huge hot tub. "What's going on? Why are you so upset?" he asked with compassion in his eyes as he leaned on the side of the hot tub.

Jane swallowed hard. "Well, I have something to ask you. Are you … still in love with Talia?"

Marty was taken aback. "What? My ex-wife? Are you serious, Jane? Tell me you're kidding right now."

Jane shook her head. "I'm not kidding. I saw a photo of her in your wallet."

Marty started laughing. "There's a photo of her in my wallet? I've had this wallet for twenty years. And probably haven't cleaned it out in as many years. I must've forgotten about it. I promise you I had no idea it was there."

Jane wiped her tears, feeling slightly better. "OK, but what about when you would talk about her constantly when we started dating? You weren't over her."

Marty hopped into the hot tub, fully clothed, and sat next to Jane. "Jane, I wasn't talking about Talia. I was just telling you about what my life was like before I met you. It just so happened that Talia was a part of that life. You're the only person I want to spend the rest of my life with. You. Not Talia. You and only you," Marty said as he put his arm around Jane and planted a kiss on her lips.

Jane sighed happily then started laughing. "You're soaked. I can't believe you came in here fully clothed."

Marty's eyes widened as he suddenly remembered something. "Speaking of my wallet, I'm pretty sure all my credit cards and cash are wet now," he said, standing up to pull it out of his back pocket.

CHAPTER NINE

Early Monday morning, after eating breakfast pizzas made by Greg using the pizza oven at the Victorian, the ladies headed out in skirts and heels for their last dancing lesson before the competition.

"I'm so stuffed. How am I going to dance?" Sarah asked as she put her hand on her stomach.

"You're telling me. I never knew breakfast pizzas existed, but I think I'm hooked. What was all on top besides eggs and sausage?" Donna asked.

"Cheese, some potatoes and scallions. Pretty sure he threw on some fresh basil too. I'm married to the guy, and I've *never* had that pizza until this morning," Liz said as they continued to walk.

Margaret laughed. "Well, let's burn off these calories during the dance lesson."

"That's the goal," Lisa said with a wink.

They got to the gates of the courtyard and walked through to find the dance instructors doing a choreographed dance to fast-paced music.

Lisa widened her eyes. "Wow. Looks like they've been practicing that for a while."

More students filed in behind them until they were all surrounding the dance floor, clapping and cheering for their instructors.

Natalia picked up a microphone as the dancers finished and stepped off the dance floor. "Testing. Testing. Alright, everyone. I've got a microphone now. Much better than that megaphone. What you saw there is a little something we're adding to the beginning of the competition. The guys have been working on it this morning."

"This morning? That's it?" Margaret asked.

Donna chuckled. "Looks like it."

Natalia was back on the microphone. "We can begin lessons. Pair up with your instructor and let's get this show on the road. We have the competition this evening."

Vinny walked up to Margaret, toweling the sweat off his face. "We've got a lot of work to do. I hope you're ready to dance," he said, whipping the towel onto the ground.

Margaret stared at the towel sitting crumpled on the grass. "Oh ... uh ... OK then. I'm ready."

The music started and Vinny put his hand in Margaret's and the other one around her back. "Let's begin. One, two, three ..." he said while they proceeded to do the box step together.

Margaret turned her head to see what her friends were doing. Each pair traveled all over the dance floor doing the box step as well. Donna winked at her.

"Margaret, eyes here," Vinny said matter-of-factly.

Margaret turned her eyes to Vinny, but she couldn't help but look back over at her friends and sister after hearing one of them laughing. It appeared Lisa was having the time of her life as her dance instructor cracked jokes left and right.

"Margaret, I'm not going to tell you twice," Vinny said sternly.

Margaret froze, feeling like she was in grade school again. It was just like getting reprimanded by a teacher, and she wasn't sure how to respond. Had she been disrespectful to Vinny? Or was he being inappropriate with his response? Before she had too much time to think it over, Vinny had them box-stepping across the dance floor, maneuvering around the other couples.

Liz and her instructor danced near Margaret and Vinny. "How's it going?" Liz asked.

Margaret widened her eyes at Liz signaling something was up, but then stepped on Vinny's foot.

Vinny stopped their dance in the middle of the dance floor. "Margaret, you need to pay attention. How are you ever going to learn this dance if your eyes are everywhere except where they need to be? You're stepping on my feet. Your posture is terrible. Honestly, we aren't going to win this competition if you don't put in the work."

Margaret crinkled her nose, feeling frustration and embarrassment at the same time. "This competition is for fun, Vinny. Fun. How much can I possibly learn in two lessons? Don't you think you're taking this a little *too* seriously?"

The other couples overheard the conversation and turned to listen as they danced from corner to corner on the dance floor around Margaret and Vinny.

Vinny stared at Margaret. "*Just* for fun? I'll have you know that we travel around the world putting on this competition. Yes, it's for beginners, but I take my job seriously."

Margaret was at loss for words. She looked over at Sarah, who appeared to have the sweetest instructor, then at Liz who had her instructor laughing after she mistakenly stepped the wrong way. Here, Margaret had an instructor with two sides, an overly flirty dance partner and a drill sergeant.

Vinny scooped her back up before she could say anything and they were back to working on the box step, awkwardly for Margaret, that's for sure.

"Elbows, Margaret! Elbows!" Vinny said as they danced around the floor.

Margaret fixed her elbows and flashed her wedding ring accidentally in the process.

"Married?" Vinny asked.

"Yes, I am," Margaret said proudly.

Vinny laughed. "Well, can he do *this*?" he asked as he dipped Margaret low and pulled her back up right into the box step.

Margaret sighed, not overly impressed with anything he had just done, but she continued on, as she wasn't one to not finish something she started. As they danced, Margaret misplaced her footing, causing her to almost stumble over Vinny. Instead of laughing it off, Vinny looked like a kettle ready to blow.

The hour was up, and the music stopped. Natalia was back on the microphone. "OK, everyone. Make sure to wear a black skirt or slacks for the competition. Don't forget to invite your family and friends, and let's have some fun. See you at 6 p.m."

The ladies walked through the gates of the courtyard, their feet feeling sore again. Margaret took off her heels, walking barefoot up the sidewalk back to the Victorian.

"Gino, my dance instructor, was hilarious today. Everything he said had me cracking up," Lisa said.

"Tony was the same. Great guy," Liz said.

Donna nodded in agreement. "Today was a lot of fun. It definitely looked like we were all doing the waltz out there."

"What was going on with you and Vinny?" Sarah asked. "Looked like he was critiquing you *a lot*."

Margaret shook her head. "He turned into a different person today. Yesterday he was awkwardly flirty, but today he was kind of *mean*. I didn't have fun at this lesson *at all*. I couldn't wait for it to be over."

"Oh no," Liz said as she put her hand on Margaret's shoulder.

"Why don't you ask Natalia to find you someone else to dance with?" Lisa said.

Margaret shrugged. "I thought about it, but what is she going to do? Swap me out with someone else's partner? Then that person will have to deal with him, and I'll feel horrible. I can't do that. Plus, it's too late. Let's just do this competition and get it over with."

Donna bit her lip. "We don't have to do this competition, you know? I'm fine with skipping it. It's not a big deal to me."

Liz, Sarah, and Lisa all nodded in agreement.

"No. You all are not skipping the competition because of me. We're all going tonight, and it'll be fun regardless of how well we do. I'll just ignore Vinny and focus on my steps. We'll have the guys come and support us, and then afterwards, have us a fabulous evening."

* * *

"Judy, hand me those pink roses, please," Bertha said from atop a ladder as she wove flowers into the arch that Marty and Jane would be married under.

Tracy held the bottom of the ladder steady in the sand on the beach, while Judy reached into the bucket full of pink roses and handed a few to Bertha.

Carol stood on another ladder, twisting white fabric around the arch, careful not to touch the flowers. "This wind is really picking up," she said as the fabric blew in her face.

Linda shielded her eyes from the blowing sand as she set up chairs around the arch.

Tracy glanced at the chairs. "Linda, this is going to be a quick ceremony. So, we only need about seven chairs set up for those that won't be able to stand for too long like Gertrude."

"Got it," Linda said as she positioned the last chair.

"Anyone know the weather report? Is this wind supposed to let up by the time the ceremony starts at noon?" Judy asked, feeling a little concerned.

Bertha shrugged. "I'm not sure, but when the option to

have the ceremony inside was presented to Jane, she balked at the idea. She's dead set on having it out here, wind or not. So, we'll do what we can."

Inside, Jane had her closest friends and sisters with her as she donned her wedding dress in the main suite on the top floor, while Marty was with his friends and some cousins getting ready a floor down.

Bob and the rest of the guys were in charge of clearing tables so catering had a place to set up as well as helping the band get situated by the pool for the reception.

By eleven, the guests had arrived and were mingling in the house and outside on the decks, awaiting the start of the wedding, when Bertha walked out of the room that Jane was in and closed the door behind her. Looking at the guests around her with smile, she said, "She's ready. It's time for everyone to gather outside on the beach for the ceremony."

Once outside, the group crowded behind the arch, facing the ocean. The wind had died down a little, and it appeared the weather was going to work out after all.

Marty stood under the arch with their pastor, awaiting his bride, smiling and holding back tears.

The violinist started playing and down the beach path walked Jane and her father. Jane had on fancy sandals, but her father insisted on wearing his oxfords with his suit.

"Oh my goodness, Jane is beautiful," Judy said as she nudged Bob. "How perfect of a day is this for a wedding," she said as she snapped some photos with her cell phone.

Just as Jane's father was about to hand her off to Marty, a huge wind gust lifted the arch into the air and dropped it fifteen feet away, loosening the flowers and sending them flying everywhere.

"Oh no!" Bertha yelled.

Marty shielded Jane as they hurried up the beach path. Her perfectly styled hairdo had come undone and stood straight up. Marty tried to fix it for her, but there was no use.

The wind continued to ruin any progress he made. "You look beautiful, Jane. Absolutely stunning," he said as he held his suit jacket over her head to stop the wind from inflicting further damage.

Jane forced a laugh from under the jacket. "As do you, my Marty, but our guests look like they've been through a wind tunnel, and our arch and decorations are probably floating in the ocean. Let's go inside and get this done. I'm ready to be man and wife," she said, taking his hand. Then she yelled back over her shoulder, "Follow us, everyone."

The guests quickly chased down what could be salvaged of the flowers and put them back in the buckets of water on the deck while Bertha and Tracy fished the arch out of the tide and brought it back near the pool.

By the time everyone got situated in the upstairs areas where the living room, kitchen, and dining room were, Marty and Jane were more than ready for their nuptials.

The room was quiet as Marty slipped a ring on Jane's finger. "Jane, words can't explain how happy I was the day you came into my life. Since that day—"

Knock. Knock.

Everyone stared down the stairs, unsure what they'd just heard.

"Continue on, son. It was probably the wind," Tracy said.

Marty looked Jane in the eyes again. "Since that day—"

Knock. Knock. Knock.

This time they all heard it, and it was definitely someone knocking.

"Who could be knocking on the door?" Judy asked, feeling frustrated for Marty and Jane.

Suddenly the door downstairs swung open. "Hello! Catering is here! Anyone home?"

Charles slapped his forehead. "I forgot to let catering know that they can't set up yet. Hold on, I'll go down and take care of it," he said as he hurried down the steps.

A few minutes later, Charles was back, and the room was quiet again.

Marty took a deep breath and squeezed Jane's hand. "Since that day, I've been—"

Beep. Beep. Beep. Beep. Beep.

"What now?" Charles interrupted. He looked out the window to see the band's van backing up into the driveway, hence the beeping.

"I'll be right back," Charles said as he started going down the steps.

Marty held his hand up. "Dad, just wait. It won't take long."

Miraculously, by then the van had stopped backing in, the beeping had halted, and the wind had died down. You could hear a pin drop in the huge Outer Banks house.

Marty looked deep into Jane's eyes, squeezing her hands tight. "Since that day, I've never had a bad day because you were by my side. You have made me the happiest I've ever been, and I can't wait to call you my wife. In my eyes, you are perfect, and you make life wonderful."

Jane wiped tears from her eyes and smiled. "Marty, I feel the same exact way about you. You are the man of my dreams, and every day I get to spend with you, I thank my lucky stars."

The pastor quickly stepped in with some words and pronounced them man and wife.

Everyone cheered loudly as Marty and Jane kissed, then more knocking came at the downstairs door.

Marty laughed. "Let them in! We are husband and wife —*finally*!"

The guests whooped and hollered and laughed as the wedding cake was delivered by the delivery guy and placed on the dining room table.

"Did I come at a bad time?" the delivery guy asked awkwardly, noticing something had been going on in the room he was standing in. "I was told the wedding was outside on the beach."

Jane laughed. "The wind kind of ruined that plan. We just got married here a few minutes ago."

"Oh, I'm so sorry. Did I interrupt?" the guy asked.

"Not at all. You came at the perfect time, actually," Marty said as he put his arm around Jane and gave her a kiss.

Bob glanced outside, then turned to everyone else. "Looks like the wind is gone. Nothing but blue skies and sunshine out there."

Jane clapped her hands. "Perfect! Why don't we head out there so catering can set up. Soon enough, the band should be ready to play."

CHAPTER TEN

"So, he's coming here?" Margaret asked as she searched around the Victorian for the cheap water shoes she'd bought at the drugstore.

Lisa smiled and shrugged. "He said he wanted to pick me up and that whoever else wanted to could catch a ride."

Sarah laughed. "Guess he remembered your phone number on the beach, huh?"

"I'm as shocked as you," Lisa blushed.

Greg dangled his keys. "I'll take the rest of us," he said as he headed outside and started the car.

Just then, Lisa looked out the window to see a refurbished baby-blue vintage Ford Bronco with the top off. "He's here, and he has a cooler car than I do."

"Oh, I'm getting in that. I love a summer drive with the top down," Donna said as she led the way outside.

Donna, Dale, Dave, Margaret and Lisa all hopped into Nick's Bronco and Sarah, Chris, Liz, and Greg piled into Greg's car and followed behind Nick to Highs Beach.

Nick smiled at Lisa in the passenger seat, then looked in his rearview mirror. "Hi, everyone. Don't mind the mess in here. There's sand everywhere from surfing yesterday."

"Hi, Nick. Thanks so much for taking us on this little adventure. We're looking forward to it," Margaret yelled over the wind that whipped her hair everywhere.

"Great Bronco. I'm a little jealous," Dave yelled out as he looked the interior over.

Nick smiled in the rearview. "Thank you. She sure is fun."

"How long does it take to get to Highs Beach?" Dale loudly asked.

"I would say about twenty minutes. You all brought shoes for walking in the sand and water, right?" Nick asked as he glanced again at Lisa with a smile.

Donna and Dale nodded. "Sure did."

"Perfect. Since we can't hear each other very well with the wind, I'm going to put some music on until we get there," he said turning the radio up to a song playing on the '70s station.

Twenty minutes later, they pulled down a quiet side road full of small modest houses. Nick drove to the end and found a spot in front of a dilapidated house. Greg parked behind him.

They all got out and stood in a circle on the road.

Lisa smiled as she glanced at Nick while he talked with the others. He looked more gorgeous than ever. His baseball cap let out some strands of his blond hair underneath, and his tan arms looked so defined under his white T-shirt. His tall stature —at a massive six foot four—was dreamy too. Not only that, but he was polite and courteous to her friends, making sure they felt comfortable on the drive there.

Nick cleared his throat as he looked out towards the bay and back towards the group. "So, we call this the mudflats or sandbars. The best time to come out is at low tide. When, it's low, gullies form between the sandbars, and you can see so much nature out here. Now, down about a quarter mile to the right is our other oyster farm. We'll head that way now," he said leading everyone down to the sandbars.

As they walked, it felt like they entered a different state or even planet. They could see miles of sandbars with gullies all around them. Nobody else was around—it was as though this little slice of heaven wasn't exactly well known to anyone but the oyster farmers.

Nick bent down and pointed to thousands of tiny green balls in some shallow water on the sand. "See these? They're everywhere. These are horseshoe crab eggs."

"You're kidding," Sarah said as she bent down closer to examine them.

"Oh, look, there's a turtle," Margaret yelled as she saw one walking over the sand.

Everyone stopped to watch and take photos. They'd seen plenty of turtles before but never on this terrain.

Lisa's eye was caught by some black shells submerged in a three-inch-deep water gully. "What are these, Nick? Hermit crabs?"

Nick shook his head. "Those are snails."

Chris nodded. "We have these over at the inlet near the boats where the water gets shallow."

Nick shook Chris's hand. "How you doing. That's right, you run the birding boat. You probably see a lot of this stuff daily, huh?"

Chris sighed as he looked around the expansive beach. "I do, but not sandbars and gullies like this. This is a different experience for sure. You'll have to come over to my world and get on the boat some time."

"I'd love that," Nick said as he spotted some blue herons landing ahead.

"Ah, there they are. I knew I'd see some blue herons out here eventually," Chris said with a smile.

As the group walked towards the oyster farm, many of them broke off into couples, stopping to explore and look through the water in the gullies and reeds to see what they could find.

Lisa walked alone towards a jellyfish on the sand, stopping to stare at it.

"You can touch it; it can't sting you. The stingers are on the bottom," Nick said as he walked up behind her unexpectedly.

Lisa nodded, feeling her heart flutter a little. "Didn't know that."

Nick smiled. "Do you like it out here?"

Lisa looked around. "I love it. It's oddly nostalgic."

"Good. I was hoping you'd enjoy it," Nick said, his blue eyes glistening under the rim of his baseball cap.

Lisa bit her lip. "I'm starting to remember being out here as a teenager. I think my parents got a summer rental around here when I was fifteen. Though, maybe it was somewhere else. Those years are so foggy sometimes. Did you discover all of this after setting up your oyster farm?"

Nick shook his head, then pointed towards a small weathered house up near the street with brown shingles. "That there was my grandparents' house. They sold it to someone else twenty years ago, but I spent my summers there. As kids, we'd come out here and go clamming and crabbing. It was just daily exploring and fun."

"That sounds amazing. I do remember some boys teaching my sister and I how to clam one summer ..." Lisa said as they walked towards the oyster farm.

"Weird. I wonder if it was me and my brother?" Nick asked as he mulled it over.

Lisa laughed. "I doubt it. We would remember each other, wouldn't we?"

Nick bit his lip. "Lisa. Do I remember a Lisa ...?"

Suddenly, his eyes widened, and he stopped and stared at Lisa. He pulled off his baseball cap, revealing his blond hair. "Do I look familiar?"

Lisa looked him in the eyes, trying to rack her brain, then shook her head. "I don't think so."

Nick put his hat back on. "Guess it was someone else. For a minute there—"

Lisa widened her eyes and pointed ahead. "Is that the oyster farm? All those racks near the water?"

Nick smiled. "Yep," he said as he turned around to see the rest of the group right beside them. As they approached, Nick gestured to hundreds of mesh bags on trestles sitting on the beach just above the water. Inside of them were oysters. "Well, here it is. We use the rack and bag culture method out here. The oysters grow and feed inside the bags, which protect them from predators," Nick said as everyone stared in fascination, none of them ever having seen an oyster farm before.

Nick pointed towards the houses sitting high up on the road. "Low tide is when we can get out here. When it's high tide, the water goes up to around five feet all the way to the houses there. It's pretty neat to watch the transformation out here, though it takes hours."

Lisa caught Nick's eye and smiled at him. Nick smiled back. "If you ever want to come out here for sunset, just say the word," he said directly to Lisa.

As the group spent some time walking around the oyster farm, Nick stepped away from the others and stood next to Lisa as she looked inside a gully filled with six inches of water. "See anything good?" he asked.

Lisa jumped. "Oh, you scared me," she said with a chuckle. "I'm watching this crab walk around."

Nick squatted to get a closer look. "That's a blue claw."

"You really know your stuff, huh?" Lisa asked, impressed.

Nick shrugged. "I like to think I do," he said as he flashed a smile. "Why don't you tell me more about yourself?"

Lisa smiled. "Well, what did you want to know?"

Nick sighed as he sat down on a dry piece of sand and got comfortable. "Well, let's start with the basics. What do you do for a living?"

Lisa nodded. "Well, I work for myself. I run an online surf shop."

Nick widened his eyes in disbelief. "You're kidding! How are you just telling me this now?"

Lisa shrugged and laughed. "You never asked."

Nick sighed. "I guess I was too busy talking about what I do here on the oyster farm," he said holding his arms out wide.

"Well, running an oyster farm is such a unique career. I think it's fascinating … but why are you working over at the oyster bar? Aren't you busy with the farm?" Lisa asked.

"Right. Right," Nick said, understanding Lisa's point. "Well, it took some time before we had enough restaurants buying from the farm to make a full-time living of it. So, I worked both jobs, and even after the farm became successful, I decided to stay at Joe's. I don't think I'll be there for too much longer, though, as I don't get much time for days off. But I enjoy the socialization I get out of working there, like how I met you."

Lisa blushed. "That's true. Are you divorced?" she blurted out.

Nick laughed. "That … I am not. I've been quite the bachelor most of my life."

Lisa chuckled. "Oh, I know your kind … enjoying the luxury of being single. I get it."

Nick shrugged. "I guess I was a bit of an oddball. Or maybe it was that I never found anyone worth settling down with. Why did you and your husband split?"

Lisa paused for a moment in thought. "Well, I don't know if I should get into all of that. It was quite a messy divorce."

"Oh, really? Well, don't feel like you have to," Nick said as he looked off into the distance.

"Let's just say my husband at the time had a whole other family outside of our marriage that I didn't know about. A wife and twin babies on the other side of the island. Somehow it took me two years to discover this. I'm guessing with how busy I was starting up my business. Anyway, the other woman didn't know about me either. We both left him. It probably didn't faze him. I assume he went off and immediately started a new family with someone else," Lisa said as she looked away, feeling annoyed that she was even talking about her ex.

"I'm … so sorry. I guess now I see why you had to leave Hawaii," Nick said as he stared at Lisa, pain filling his eyes on her behalf.

Lisa shrugged. "Don't be sorry. It's over. Thankfully, we never had kids, so I never have to see or talk to him again. But it really makes me understand why someone would choose to be single … like yourself," Lisa said, feeling slightly jaded.

Nick bit his lip. "Well, I've grown a bit since then. I'm forty-eight now. I think it might be time to settle down soon. Being a bachelor is getting old," he said as he stared into Lisa's eyes with a smile. It felt like he was looking directly into her soul as they shared a long glance, both wondering what the other was thinking.

Lisa looked away. "Settling down, eh?"

Nick laughed. "Well, I'm not looking to get hitched tomorrow. I guess I mean to just find someone I can build a life with. Anyway, tell me about this online surf shop. I'm intrigued."

Lisa bent down to study the gully and swished her hand through the water as she looked at her reflection. "I started the company on my own when I was living in Hawaii. My husband-at-the-time wasn't involved. It's beach-themed clothing, shoes, and surfboards that I helped design. I have a factory here in the United States that makes the products and a warehouse that handles the order fulfillment and shipping."

"I'm blown away by this," Nick said as she shook his head and smiled at Lisa in disbelief. "Tell me more. What else do I need to know about you?"

Lisa sat on the sand next to Nick and stretched her legs out. "Well, here's something else. I'm not sure how long I'll be in Cape May. I came here on a whim, but I think I caught the van-life bug. I can see myself heading off on the open road and seeing all the beauty this country has to offer."

Nick diverted his eyes. "Oh … really? Where would you go next?"

Lisa shrugged and smiled. "I guess it all depends on what happens in Cape May while I'm here."

Nick nodded as he looked at Lisa, then there it was … their eyes locked and he felt himself slowly leaning into her ….

"Hey, guys. Whatcha doing over here?" Liz asked as the group stood over them.

Nick quickly stood up and wiped the sand off his shorts. "Just having a quick chat. Hey, are you guys hungry by chance?" Nick asked as he helped Lisa up off the sand.

Margaret looked at Dave and nodded. "I know we are."

"Us too," Sarah said, as everyone else in the group nodded.

"Well, I know the perfect restaurant right on the bay if you feel like heading back for lunch on the house," Nick said with a smile.

"Oh, I'm down for Joe's Oyster Bar any day, but please don't feel the need to pay for us," Dale said.

Nick waved his hand in the air. "I would like to pay for you all. I always treat my friends when they visit Joe's, and I think I consider you all friends at this point."

"Well, that is so sweet of you," Margaret said as she reached for Dave's hand. "Thank you, Nick."

"Perfect. Let's head back before the tide starts creeping in," Nick said as he placed his hand on the small of Lisa's back, making every part of her body tingle.

CHAPTER ELEVEN

"One. Two. One. Two. Three. Four," the lead singer of the band said into the microphone as the rest of the bandmates warmed up their instruments.

"Well, the band is ready," Linda said as she stood next to Mike and Judy outside.

The lead singer started on the first verse, then stopped. "Alright, one more time. From the beginning," he said turning to the guitarist.

Mike chuckled. "I think they probably needed to do a sound check, but it doesn't look like they have much time for that."

Judy looked to the upper deck. "How's catering going inside?"

Linda shrugged. "I'm guessing OK, but we're not up there. We got delegated the band. Not sure how much help we can be with them, though."

The music stopped, and the lead singer looked back at the drummer. "You're timing is all off, Ralph. Let's start over ...."

Ralph threw his drumstick. "My timing isn't off, yours is, *Doug.*"

Linda shifted her eyes. "Any of you know the drums? I

think Ralph is ready to drive that van back to wherever they came from. *Alone.*"

Judy laughed. "That's a no."

Just then, Bob walked out onto the upper deck. "Judy ... um ... can you come up here, please? Maybe Linda too. Heck, all of you. Come up here," he said waving his arms.

"Uh-oh. This doesn't sound good," Mike said as he led the way up the steps to the second floor.

Once inside, they saw the catering displayed beautifully on the long kitchen table and island, but everyone was running around frantically.

"What can we help with?" Judy asked Bob as he pulled open a kitchen drawer and promptly shut it.

Debbie interrupted. "Catering set up all of this, left, and forgot to put the burners under the chafing dishes."

Linda shook her head. "Call them and tell them to get back here with the burners, then."

Carol rolled her eyes as she looked around the room. "We did. They aren't answering. I feel like they may have left them in a bag around here somewhere."

Marty and Jane appeared from the downstairs, happy and oblivious as could be.

"Oh the food looks amazing," Jane said as she scooped some baked ziti onto a little plate. "I know we're not all ready, but I'm sneaking this. I'm hungry. Don't mind me," she said as she and Marty walked outside onto the deck.

Bob nudged Judy and muttered under his breath. "Do we tell them?"

Judy shook her head. "No. It was already bad enough with that wind ruining the outdoor ceremony."

Linda looked at Mike. "Do you mind running out and getting thirty burners? We don't have much time before this food is ice cold."

Mike grabbed his keys off the counter and headed out the door. "I'm on it, hon."

"Wait for me. I'm going too," Bob said as he glanced at Judy before booking it down the steps to meet Mike outside.

Judy sighed as she started putting the lids back on the chafing dishes. "We have to keep these warm. This should do the trick for now."

Just then, the door burst open and in came a large group of the wedding guests who'd been outside mingling.

Debbie waved her arms in the air. "Hey, everyone. The food isn't ready yet up here. There is an appetizer table by the pool, though."

Linda glanced at Carol. "Thankfully, they are cold appetizers that don't need warmers."

Thirty minutes later, Mike and Bob were back with warmers, and everyone quickly stepped in to get them lit and under the chafing dishes.

Linda sighed as she flopped onto a chair. "Phew. That was a close one. Now how's the band—"

Suddenly the door flew open from the deck, and Bertha appeared, huffing and puffing, having run up two flights of steps. "*Who* booked this band?"

Everyone in the room shrugged.

"What's going on *now*?" Judy asked.

Bertha shook her head. "They have yet to finish a song, and they're all arguing. It's awkward."

Linda laughed at the absurdity of the situation as she stayed laid back on the chair. "They were doing that before we came up here. I'm guessing Marty and Jane booked them."

Loud music started playing behind Bertha. "Oh, maybe they worked their kinks out *finally*," she said turning around and heading back down the steps.

Judy stepped out onto the deck. "Hey, everyone. Catering is ready," she yelled just after the band finished their song.

All the guests had apparently been waiting on the food as they all promptly came inside to make plates.

After ensuring the plates, silverware, and napkins were

stocked, Judy, Linda, Bob, and Mike all headed outside to the pool where the band performed for the three guests who hadn't gone inside to eat.

Judy watched as the guitarist bent over and turned up the speaker volume mid-song.

"Do you think Marty and Jane are enjoying themselves?" Linda yelled over the music.

"What?" Judy yelled back.

Linda leaned inches away from Judy's ear, still yelling. "Marty and Jane. Think they're having fun?"

Judy still couldn't hear her, but she made out a few words. "Yes, I think so," she said, noticing the neighbors were now standing on their decks staring towards them with scowls on their faces.

Judy nudged Linda and pointed to the neighbors. "I think the music is too loud for them."

Linda laughed. "It's too loud for *us*."

"Should we say something to the band?" Judy asked.

Linda shrugged. "I'm afraid to say anything. What if they start arguing again because of it? I don't want to be the one responsible for getting the band off track again."

Judy nodded. "You're right."

Just then, Tracy and Bertha appeared, holding their ears. Bertha marched right over to the band. "Turn down the speakers. It's way too loud. We're going to get the cops called on us," she said to Doug.

Doug shook his head. "What? Turn down the music?" he asked between the lyrics he was singing. "This is the volume we always play at."

Tracy pushed Bertha aside. "Look, Mr. Lead Singer. If the cops come here due to a noise complaint and ruin this wedding for Marty and Jane, you will have to deal with *me*."

Doug rolled his eyes and leaned over to turn the speaker down to a more acceptable volume. It was still quite loud, but at least you could hear the person next to you now.

As the guests started filing outside with their plates of food, it became quite crowded around the pool area.

Judy found two empty recliner lounge chairs away from all the chaos and took a seat with Bob. Bob held her hand in his as they watched Marty and Jane dancing to the band with the guests starting to join them.

Judy sighed with relief. "Look at them. They're loving the band. Smiling and dancing."

Bob nodded. "Glad to see it after the debacle earlier," he said with a chuckle. "Want to go join them?"

"In a few minutes. I need to sit for a little bit," Judy said as she continued to watch everyone dance and sing.

Suddenly there was a big splash and some screaming. Then, the music cut off.

"What happened? I can't see anything," Judy asked as she stood up from the chair and tried to look around the many people blocking the pool. Finally, she got a glimpse of the spectacle. There, in the pool, were Marty and Jane. They had fallen in while dancing.

Linda pushed her way through the guests to Judy and Bob. "Did you see what happened?" she asked, horrified.

"Yes," Judy said as she watched Marty and Jane get out of the pool and grab towels another guest had brought them.

Marty pointed to the band and yelled out. "Keep the music playing! The party is just getting started!" Then, he wrapped his arms around Jane and dipped her for a kiss. They both laughed then made their way back towards the band and started dancing again like nothing had happened.

Judy held her chest. "Well, looks like everything is OK. Wet but OK."

Mike pushed through the crowds and motioned to Bob, Judy, and Linda to follow him.

"Now what?" Linda asked, feeling exasperated.

"Let's get out there and dance already," Mike said.

Linda looked at Judy and laughed. "It's time."

* * *

Around two o'clock, Nick drove the group to Joe's Oyster Bar with Greg following behind them.

Nick looked at Lisa with a smile as he put the Bronco in park, then held his finger up. "Wait here one minute," he said as he hurried inside the restaurant.

Moments later, Nick was back with a smile plastered on his face. "Got us a cozy table in the back. Ready to head in?"

"Perfect, I'm starving," Margaret said as Dave helped her out of the vehicle.

"Us too," Liz said as she got out of Greg's car.

Jeremy, the owner, waited by the host stand with menus for their group. "Follow me this way," he said, glancing at Lisa with a smile. He led the way through the rustic restaurant to a back table in a dark corner lit by tealight candles.

Everyone sat down, thoroughly impressed with the table Nick snagged for them.

Dale looked over the menu, along with everyone else, then set it down and cleared his throat. "So, the dance competition is tonight at 6 p.m., right?"

Donna thought for a moment. "Yes, it is. I figured you guys can meet us there, and then we can head out to dinner somewhere."

Dale nodded. "That should work fine for us, right fellas?"

Dave, Greg, and Chris all nodded.

"Do you all feel you're ready to dance the waltz?" Chris asked.

Margaret bobbed her head side to side. "I think so. Though, I can't stand the guy I'm dancing with."

Sarah, Lisa, Donna, and Liz all groaned, "Vinny."

Margaret nodded. "He's just … quite the character. I'll leave it at that."

Dave widened his eyes. "Well, I guess I'll finally meet this *character* tonight."

Margaret rolled her eyes and chuckled. "I'm looking forward to *that* meeting."

Greg glanced at the end of the table at Nick, who was seated across from Lisa. "Thank you for giving us a tour of the oyster farm today, Nick."

Nick waved his hand. "Oh, it was nothing. I enjoyed showing you guys around."

Liz smiled. "And we love this place. Perfect choice for dinner."

Nick nodded and smiled. "No problem."

Just then, the waiter came by with baskets of hot toasty bread and delivered glasses of ice waters for everyone.

Dale snapped his fingers. "We forgot to stop and get some wine."

Nick glanced out the window. "There's actually a little bar next door that sells some."

"Perfect. I'll go grab something. Wine, ladies?" Dale asked.

"Yes, please. Maybe a sauvignon blanc?" Donna said as she glanced at the ladies for a response. They all nodded.

When Dale stood to leave, the rest of the guys decided to join him, which left just the women at the table.

Donna turned to Margaret, Sarah, Liz, and Lisa. "Did any of you tell the guys what time the dance competition was? Because I didn't."

They all looked at each other and shook their heads.

"I didn't," Sarah said as she ripped a piece of the bread and spread some butter on it.

Margaret tried to rack her brain. "Maybe I did? I can't remember, but I don't think so."

Sarah thought for a moment. "Did anyone tell Chris we were doing the waltz? I was keeping that a secret from him. Wanted to surprise him when they came to watch us."

Everyone shook their head.

"I knew you wanted to surprise Dale, so I was pretty vague

with Greg about our dance," Liz said as she took a bite of the bread.

Donna scratched her head. "Well, something fishy is going on here ..."

Liz and Margaret exchanged glances, not sure of what to say to Donna.

"We're back," Dale said as the guys approached the table holding some chilled wine bottles.

"Perfect. Thank you, dear," Donna said with a smile.

Nick took his seat across from Lisa. They looked at each other for a lingering moment, then smiled at the same time.

"It's a neat little place next door. I'll have to show you it sometime," Nick said.

Lisa nodded. "I'm down for that."

While the rest of the table chatted, Nick grew nervous, unsure of what to say to Lisa. "You look nice," he finally said.

Lisa blushed and looked down at her white shirt. "Oh jeez, this is what I consider hiking clothes. I didn't want to wear anything I liked too much today with all the sand, water, and mud."

Nick shrugged. "Well, you look really nice in your hiking clothes."

Lisa laughed. "And you look great as well."

Nick rolled his eyes. "OK, now you're pulling my leg."

Lisa took a sip from the wineglass Donna passed her, then set it down. "No, you're pretty handsome, Nick."

Nick's entire face turned red, and he stared at Lisa, smiling. "Well, thank you. You're pretty gorgeous yourself."

Lisa shook her head and laughed at the absurdity of the situation. They were both obviously into the other, but it was taking forever to directly say that.

"What are you doing tonight?" Nick asked.

"We have this dance competition tonight at six, but other than that, I don't think there's set plans," Lisa said.

"That's right. Donna just mentioned the dance competition, and I remember you bringing it up out on the waves. What's that all about?" Nick asked, perplexed.

Lisa nodded and laughed. "Yes. It's something they're doing in Cape May. Two lessons and a competition, all in the name of fun, of course. What about you? Any plans?"

Nick shrugged and ran his fingers through his hair. "I'm off for the evening. I was thinking it'd be nice to meet up … maybe catch a sunset."

Lisa thought for moment. "Why don't you stop by the competition over at the Blackberry Hotel. I'm not sure what we're doing after, but maybe we can fit in a sunset if time allows."

"I'd like that," Nick said with a smile just as the waiter was back and ready to take everyone's order.

CHAPTER TWELVE

After the wedding reception was over, Bob and Judy packed up and hit the road.

Bob drove the car as Judy relaxed in the passenger seat.

"Are you sure you don't want to use the map?" Bob asked with a chuckle.

Judy pointed to her phone. "The GPS is all set up. Just follow it home. We don't need the map."

Bob sighed with relief as he looked in the rearview mirror, watching the Outer Banks beach house get smaller and smaller as they continued to drive. "You sure you want to leave now? We're probably going to get home around midnight. We can still turn back and leave tomorrow morning like we initially planned."

Judy nodded. "While it was a fun and certainly *action-packed* weekend, I'm ready to be in my own home, in our own bed. Plus, I can't wait to see Hugo. Hopefully, he enjoyed hanging at Liz and Greg's all weekend with Greg's parents."

Bob nodded. "I'm glad you wanted to leave early … because I did too, though I didn't tell you that. I know it was important for you to be there for Marty's wedding."

Judy laughed. "Oh, I had a feeling you wanted to leave

early. Next time we go to the Outer Banks, I'll make sure we have a room that suits us."

Bob rubbed his back. "It's probably going to take a week to get these knots out of my back from that horrible bed." He glanced at Judy. "Do you think Marty and Jane enjoyed their wedding?"

Judy paused for a moment in thought. "I sure hope so. Nothing went according to plan, but they seemed to be enjoying themselves. If anything, it made for a memorable day."

Bob laughed. "Can't say there was anything boring about their wedding, that's for sure."

Judy sighed and closed her eyes. "I'm going to rest. I didn't get much sleep at all last night due to all the running around for the wedding. Wake me up when it's my turn to drive. It's crazy, but I'm more excited to get back to Cape May then I was to get to the Outer Banks."

"Well, as the saying goes … Home sweet home. There's nothing better," Bob said with a smile as he turned up the volume on his audiobook.

* * *

Margaret, Liz, Sarah, Donna, and Lisa sashayed down the sidewalk in their long black skirts, black blouses, and heels towards the courtyard at the Blackberry Hotel.

"I can hear the music already," Sarah said as she cocked her head.

"I can't believe we're really doing this," Donna said, a smile overcoming her face.

Liz cracked her knuckles. "I'm nervous. People are going to be watching us dance?"

Margaret shrugged. "I'm more nervous about Dave watching me dance," she said with a laugh.

As they approached the gates to the courtyard, they stopped, shocked by what was in front of them.

"Is that our dance floor?" Lisa asked, staring at a dance floor that was now on a raised stage four feet off the ground.

Sarah's mouth dropped open. "They weren't kidding when they said they take this competition seriously."

A metal trussing that held moving lights in all different colors had been erected over the dance floor. White curtains attached to the truss had been strung up to act as a backdrop. The tall evergreens that bordered the courtyard made it shaded enough that the lights popped even during daylight.

A worker sat on the stage setting up a fog machine. He muttered some words before smacking the machine, causing plumes of fog to come out. He coughed and stepped back as the stage became engulfed in fog.

Natalia stood on the stage and waved her hands through the fog. "Over here, ladies!"

Liz led the way towards Natalia as Margaret caught a glimpse of Vinny warming up off to the side with the other dancers.

Vinny stopped stretching and smiled at Margaret. "Are you ready to dance, my lady?" he shouted for everyone to hear.

Margaret nodded through her embarrassment. "Sure am, Vinny," she said, looking at her friends with widened eyes.

Natalia had a huge grin on her face as they all approached her on the stage. "Well, do you like?" she asked, spreading her arms out, motioning to the stage and lights.

"It looks quite professional out here. We had no idea," Donna said as she looked around.

Natalia shrugged. "I like to keep it a surprise for our contestants. Sometimes word gets out from the previous year's participants, but usually it's a surprise. Now, the show is going to start with the dance instructors' routine, then you'll be paired up with your dancer, and everyone will compete simultaneously out on the dance floor. We don't have time to do individual performances."

"So, how does the judging work?" Lisa asked.

Natalia nodded. "If you're tapped on the shoulder while dancing, you're out. The last couple dancing is the winner."

"I guess I missed this, but is there a prize?" Sarah asked.

Natalia smiled. "Bragging rights. And a thousand dollars."

The ladies stepped off to the side and stared at each other.

"One thousand dollars? How did we not know this?" Margaret asked.

Donna shrugged. "Maybe since we were late to sign-ups? I imagine they went over it that day?"

Liz laughed. "Well, I'm not complaining."

Sarah searched the chairs near the stage. "What time is it?"

"It's ten minutes to six. Why?" Donna asked.

"I don't see the guys anywhere, and the show is about to start. Look, the dancers are already getting into position for their routine," Sarah said.

"I'm sure they're coming," Margaret said as she looked over to see Vinny staring at her from the stage.

By start time, a crowd of fifty or so had gathered to see the dance competition—whether they be family or friends of the dancers or just people who wanted to watch for fun.

The music came on, then the lights focused on the stage, and the professional dancers started their choreographed dance, which was actually quite good. They moved in sync and even threw in some backflips here and there.

The ladies stood among the twenty-five or so dance students off to the side of the stage, anxiously awaiting their time on the dance floor.

Natalia got back on the microphone. "OK, everyone, the moment you've been waiting for. Our dance competition begins now. Last couple left on the dance floor wins," she said as she exited the stage.

They all paired off with their dance partners and got into position, waiting for the music to start.

Vinny had his arm around Margaret's back and his hand in hers. "I hope you're ready to dance like you've never danced before."

Margaret forced a smile. "Sure am."

Vinny's face turned stern. "Good. I can't have you tripping again. I actually want to win this competition. My brother has won the last three times."

Margaret shifted her eyes. "So, you're looking to beat your brother, eh?"

Vinny laughed. "Yes, why else would I be here? I don't like dancing with amateurs. They're always stepping on my feet. My sister begged us to come be instructors at the last minute. I took that as my chance to get out here and show my stuff."

"To your brother," Margaret said while glancing back towards the crowd. Try as she might to find a familiar face, her heart sank when Dave wasn't anywhere to be found.

The music started and they began to dance. Margaret glanced over at her friends who had started the box step.

Margaret took a deep breath and started her steps, then the music suddenly cut off.

Natalia was back on the microphone. "Sorry, everyone, for the interruption, but we have some dancers that have shown up late. Give them a minute to get situated."

As Margaret turned to Natalia, a tap came behind Vinny's shoulder.

"May I step in here?" a familiar voice asked.

Vinny shook his head. "Absolutely not."

Margaret pulled away from Vinny when she saw it was Dave, then wrapped her arms around him like they hadn't seen each other in months. "I can't even tell you how glad I am to see you. What are you doing here, though?"

Dave smiled. "I'm here to dance with you."

Margaret's mouth dropped open. "You are? What …? Why?"

Dave laughed. "Man, it's been so hard keeping this secret from you this whole time."

Margaret's mouth was still open. "What secret?"

Dave glanced across the dance floor. Dale, Greg, and Chris had all surprised their ladies as well. "Dale wanted to learn how to dance for the wedding in July—you know, as a little surprise to Donna. Well, he didn't want to do it alone. He asked if we'd be interested in taking lessons with him."

"You took lessons? When?" Margaret asked, shocked.

Dave sighed. "A few days after work. Dale had an instructor come to the restaurant after it closed. Some of the cooks and servers got in on the lessons too. It was actually quite comical, but we learned a lot. Dale made us keep it a secret."

Margaret laughed. "So, how did you guys end up here?"

Dave glanced at Dale, who appeared to be telling the same story to Donna with her mouth hanging open like Margaret's. "Well, when Dale found out that you all were doing dance lessons this weekend, he decided the surprise should be moved to tonight. Then, that way, he and Donna could have time to practice together for the wedding. He tracked down Natalia's number and told her everything, and she was on board. Only problem was, we were running a little late today … Chris split his pants on the way here," he chuckled.

Margaret hugged Dave tight as she laughed when someone clearing their throat interrupted them.

"Are you two finished?" Vinny asked, looking extra annoyed.

Margaret smiled. "Thank you, Vinny for everything, but my husband will be my partner tonight."

Vinny shook his head. "Well, your *husband* hasn't been practicing the steps with you like I have. How are we going to win a competition under these circumstances?"

"I'm not worried about the competition. I'm here to have

fun," Margaret said as she took Dave's hand and led him to a spot near their friends on the dance floor.

Vinny clenched his fists and forcefully grabbed Margaret's other hand. "Well, *I* have a competition to win this evening, and I'm not letting *you* get in the way of that."

Dave calmly put his hand on Vinny's chest, causing him to back away. "Get your hand off my wife. I've got it from here, pal," he said as he glared at Vinny.

Vinny threw his hands up in the air and walked away while Dave let out a long breath to regain his composure.

As Dave got into position for the waltz, Margaret looked around at her friends. "Can you believe this?" she said to Liz, who was standing with Greg waiting for the music.

Liz shook her head. "I can't, but Donna's hunch was correct all along."

Margaret looked over at Donna, who was smiling from ear to ear. Lisa was still with her dance partner, but luckily, he was nothing like Vinny.

The music started, and they were off. Dave did the waltz with Margaret, and it felt like they were gliding effortlessly around the dance floor. It felt more natural than any of the dancing Margaret had done with Vinny.

"Look at you," Margaret said to Dave. "I'm married to a dancer."

Dave smiled as he focused on his steps. "I'm glad I could save you from *Vinny*. That guy is a nut job."

Margaret tried not to laugh, but it happened anyway.

Eventually, Margaret and Dave got a tap on the shoulder, so they walked offstage to stand alongside, Lisa, her partner, Greg and Liz, and Sarah and Chris. On the dance floor was one other dance couple and Dale and Donna.

The final tap happened, and Dale and Donna were declared the winners.

Everyone cheered as Natalia presented them with the prize.

Margaret glanced at Dave. "I'm glad it was them."

"Me too," Dave said as he squeezed Margaret's hand.

As everyone congratulated Donna and Dale on their win, Lisa's eye snagged on a tall blond in the crowd. "Nick is here," she said while smiling at him.

Sarah nudged Lisa. "Go over and talk to him! We'll see you back at the house."

Lisa and Nick walked towards each other, and it was as though nobody else in the crowd existed.

"So, you decided to come," Lisa said with a smile.

"I did. You looked great out there," Nick smiled back.

"Well, thank you. I appreciate that," Lisa blushed.

"We have some time to see the sunset still. I think it sets around eight thirty. Interested?" Nick asked.

"Definitely."

Minutes later, they were in the Bronco with top off, the wind whipping their hair as they drove twenty minutes back to Highs Beach.

After arriving, Nick pulled a towel and bag from the back seat, and they headed to a high spot by the houses where they could sit and dangle their legs off a wall.

As the sun set, Nick rubbed his hands together, trying to think of what to say. "I gave this a lot of thought last night. I think we have met before. When you stayed here that summer with your family, did your family have a white station wagon?" Nick asked.

Lisa thought for a moment. "Yes, we did."

Nick took off his hat and turned to Lisa, running his hands through his thick hair. "Are you sure I don't look familiar?"

Lisa stared at Nick when it suddenly dawned on her. "Wait ... it's you. You're him ... you're *Nick*!"

Nick laughed. "Yes, it was me. You were my first kiss. I had such a crush on you, and I was so heartbroken when I never saw you again."

Lisa's eyes widened. "I can't believe this. How did I not realize this?"

Nick shrugged. "It's been thirty-some years."

"You were my first kiss too." Suddenly, the memory of that summer in 1991 came rushing back to Lisa. "I talked about that summer for years. How my sister and I rode bikes with you and your brother up and down the road, and then we'd hang out on the porch for hours talking and watching the fireflies. Then, there were the nights where we'd watch the sunset with our dirty feet and clothes from being outside all day. It was something out of a movie. I always hoped that I'd see you at my high school, but I never did."

Nick nodded. "Same. We ended up moving to Maryland for a few years before coming back here. Gosh, I thought about you for years after that. Why'd we never think to exchange phone numbers?"

Lisa laughed. "I don't know. We were naive kids, I guess," she said with a smile as she glanced up at him.

Nick pointed towards the sky. "Look, the sun is setting."

Lisa's eyes widened as she stared out past the water. "I could watch the sun set every night. Look at how the sky turns pink, purple, orange, and red."

Nick turned to Lisa "How funny is that all these years later we're here in the same spot again," he said as he slowly leaned in for a kiss. She kissed him back, and felt like she could almost float away.

EPILOGUE

Two weeks later, the group of friends were out to dinner at Two Mile Crab House in Wildwood Crest.

Margaret cracked open her crab claw, then dipped it in melted butter and popped it into her mouth. "So, we finally got you to agree to a bachelorette party, Donna. It's not that bad, right?"

Donna laughed. "Well, I can't say no to *this* kind of bachelorette party," she said while taking a bite of her fried coconut shrimp.

"Does anyone want some of my fries?" Liz asked.

Sarah grabbed a fry and took a bite. "Me."

Lisa's phone made a noise, and she set down her fork to look at it. "It's Nick."

"How's that going?" Liz asked.

Lisa smiled as though in a dreamy state. "It's going well. He's across the country in Oregon doing some research for the oyster farm. I think I miss him."

"Aw," all of the ladies said in unison.

"Enough about me, are you ready for this wedding, Donna?" Lisa asked. "I can't believe it's two weeks away."

Donna took another bite of her coconut shrimp and washed it down with some wine. "Yeah, I guess we're ready. I still need to find a dress, though," she said without any sense of urgency.

All of their eyes widened in disbelief.

"You haven't found a dress yet?" Sarah asked, shocked.

Donna took another sip of her wine. "Well, I *did* find a dress, but I decided I hated it. So, now I have to find another one. It's fine. I'm sure something will come up."

Margaret nodded. "I sure hope so. I'll keep my fingers crossed for you."

Donna shrugged. "I'm not worried about it. I'll find something. As for everything else, I think we're good. We have tents coming in the day before, a DJ, photographer, and catering. I'm really trying to not get too stressed about it all. I want to relax and enjoy the process."

Sarah bit her lip. "Do you think having the wedding so soon after the engagement has been a little difficult?"

"Probably," Donna said as she grabbed one of Liz's fries.

"Well, what made you want to hurry the nuptials along?" Lisa asked.

Donna sighed and rested her chin in her hands. "I'm just totally and completely in love with Dale, and it only gets stronger every day. I want that man as my husband *yesterday*."

Sarah dabbed a napkin on her eyes. "OK, that was just the most beautiful thing I've ever heard."

Margaret smiled. "Sounds like you're ready even if your dress isn't. That's what matters. If you want a girls' trip to a local boutique to look at dresses, just say the word. We'll get it done."

"Hear! Hear!" Liz said. "Well, as long as mimosas are involved and maybe brunch. You know what? Why don't we just plan this outing now?"

Everyone at the table laughed.

* * *

Pick up **Book 14** in the Cape May Series**, Cape May Magic,** to follow Margaret, Liz, the rest of the familiar bunch, and some new characters.

Visit my website at www.claudiavance.com

ABOUT THE AUTHOR

Claudia Vance is a writer of Women's Fiction and Clean Romance. She writes feel good reads that take you to places you'd like visit with characters you'd want to get to know.

She lives with her boyfriend and 2 cats in a charming small town in New Jersey, not too far from the beautiful beach town of Cape May. She worked on television shows and film sets for many years. She's an avid gardener and nature lover.

Made in United States
North Haven, CT
17 December 2023